FOLLOWING BLANK
5 DEATHS

FOLLOWING BLANK 5 DEATHS

4 Short Stories

Sid Patki

PARTRIDGE

A Penguin Random House Company

To order additional copies of this book, contact
Partridge India
000 800 10062 62
orders.india@partridgepublishing.com

www.partridgepublishing.com/india

Dedicated to My Parents, Sheetal, Ram, Vihaan and Grandma.

Special thanks to **Tushar Pathrikar, Aditya Kulkarni, Shashank Kalyankar & Ankita Shrivastava** for their tremendous moral and editorial support.

And thank you to my first readers and my beloved friends: **Mumital Farukee, Harshal Jagtap, Nikhil Bhat, Amit Raut, Nilesh patil, Shurti Hippalgoankar, Kanishka Kapoor, Alok Kulkarni, Amit Borde, Parth & Mithil Ladda, Pankaj Yadav and Nikhil Mate.**

Contents

1 FIVE 1

2 BLANK 24

3 FOLLOWING... 42

4 DRIVE 68

1

FIVE

Sitting on the detective's couch murderer replied casually "I did kill my Wife."

"I will tell you 5 instances or stories through which I have killed my wife, and you have to choose only 1 instance which is real. If you choose correctly, I will provide you all the evidences. You can then arrest me and regain your lost honour."

"What?" asked police detective.

The Murderer took out piece of paper and displayed it blank in front of him.

"I will write number of the real story out of 5 on this blank paper. Like 1 2 3 4 5. After that I will fold this paper in front of you and drop it in the envelope and place it on the table. You will listen to all the stories and you will be given some time to choose the correct number. Once you answer, you can open the envelope. If you are right, I will tell you everything and you can arrest me, but, if you chose the wrong number, you lose and it will go down as the case you could not crack. 5 stories but only 1 true number is in the envelope. I will give you 5 minutes to think after I finish my 5th story. So Choose wisely.

"Ready?" asked the murderer.

"I can see the number now?" replied the weary detective who was awakened in the middle of the night by the man who was a prime suspect in a murder.

"Yes you can, but the number would not prove anything in the courtroom. You have already failed to prove me guilty. I am a free man. Plus, it won't give you satisfaction of knowing the number by force, it will prove your incompetency and I am sure you do not want to prove yourself again that you are useless. Do you?"

"What's the guarantee that you will give me all the evidence?" asked detective.

"No Guarantee honey, it is a one sided game, let's see you if you can pull it off. So what say? Want to try your skills one last time? But you are not allowed to interrupt me. Listen to all the stories very carefully. Every story has a clue, which might help you to decide if it is true or false. After listening to all the stories, you start by 4 wrong stories justifying why it is wrong and then the final perfect true story."

"Turn around detective; let me write the number of the real story on the paper."

Dismayed, the detective stood up and turned around. After few seconds, he was again instructed to turnaround.

"You are young detective, Are you married? I guess not, so this will be a great learning experience for you, it will teach you how to spot an evil woman.",

"Ready? Here it is" murderer placed the piece of envelope on the table leaned forward and pointing finger at envelope he said "answer to your mystery lies in this envelope, so let's start."

Murder background Story:

A woman; age 35, ex stage actress was found dead in her apartment located on the 2nd floor, not far away from the downtown. The murder was reported by her husband at 7.15pm and police reached the crime scene by 7.25pm. The Door was opened to the police by her husband and he escorted the police to master bedroom where they found the corpse lying on bed with a knife in her heart.

After the investigation; it was found that finger print on the knife belonged to the victim, thus in a way indicating suicide. Medical report concluded the death due to stabbing. Victim was heavily drunk with the traces of marijuana in the blood and time of death was around 2pm. The apartment did not show any forced entries or exit but the window was open at the time the murder was reported. Neighbours were consulted but none of them reported any unusual activity or spotting any stranger or a suspicious person around the window or the apartment.

Eventually investigation boiled down to only 2 conclusions

1. A straightway suicide.
2. Murderer appeared through the window. Most probably it could be the husband as he was not at

office desk during the time frame of murder and victim was hardly in contact with anyone else in recent months.

Victim's husband was under microscope all along as he was the only prime suspect. Investigating through his track record it was revealed that he had mental medical history and had restraining orders for a couple of women. Detective was sure right from the day one that husband was guilty but he hardly had any proof. The only thing he had on his side was suspect was not at his office desk from 1 Pm to 3 Pm but he had not left office premises as per exit camera. Detective was confident but he could not prove him guilty or at least take him in custody on such evidence. When questioned regarding his whereabouts during the time of murder he replied he was in the office courtyard which had no camera coverage.

Digging more into the victim's life, it was revealed that she had a struggling acting career and was depressed most of her life. Married life was not up to the mark and as per close friends the couple was on the verge of divorce. Couple was childless and had very few friends' in the city and most of them were formal. As per husband, victim was depressed due to no work and had mental issue like anxiety and superiority complex.

The Detective tried his level best to solve this case and insisted on for more time to solve it. He tried every possible way but he did not have any concrete proof. Eventually, no one was found guilty and the case went unsolved. It was a great set back to the detective as it was the first defeat in his glorious career. Husband claimed the body of the wife and he requested the court that her body should be cremated as it was her dying wish. Police Authorities were totally against it but they hardly had any reason to hold the body back. Despite detective's lot of tantrums, the court favoured the Victims Will which clearly stated "I don't know if I will go to Hell or heaven but I want to be liberated by air. My salvation should be through cremation only."

After completing all the funeral formalities and gulping a couple of beers of celebrations husband rang the bell of the famous detective and requested him to let him in as he had some genuine clue regarding his wife's murder. Detective let him in. It was midnight and he asked what clue he had. Murderer offered him a puzzle of 5 stories and he had to choose 1. A last chance to prove that he still has some pride & skill left in him.

Now:

"Here are the stories. Detective! Let's start and please do not speak till I finish."

"Story 1: Blank Syringe

Before leaving for the office that day, I inserted a blank syringe in the veins of my wife around 11 am, as she was drugged and asleep. It was a cake walk. Do you know about the blank syringe, detective? It is a very simple way; you buy a syringe and without inserting any liquid inject air into the person's veins thus creating bubbles in the veins which are destined to reach the heart. Bubble blocks the supply of the blood to the heart resulting into a heart failure.

"When I came home she was long dead. I stabbed her but there was no blood flow as you know once a person is dead, blood does not flow out of body. To sort this thing out, 2 weeks back I chloroformed my lovely wife when she was high on marijuana and alcohol. I took her blood and stored it in the refrigerator. After injecting the syringe, I took out the blood bag and kept it open in the morning. Thus, blood expiring timing matched: by the time I came home blood was decomposing in the same way it could have been if I could have actually stabbed while she was alive.

"So all I had to do was stab a dead body and spill the blood from the blood bag all over her. Content of the blood bag were same marijuana and alcohol. Your doctor could not figure out the exact cause of death. He was baffled for sure, if the death was due to heart failure or stabbing. As stabbing was apparent, he mentioned cause of death due to stabbing in report and as the content of the blood were same so he did not pay lot of heed. Also, it is was very less likely he would have checked the content of the blood from her body, he assumed it came out of her heart that's where he went wrong and that's why we are having this conversation. Autopsy report claimed it was stabbing and all went wrong and for you. I was in the office courtyard" smiled the murderer.

"Once she told me why she wanted to marry me, because I was genuine which implies for boring, that I am caring which implies for her own butler and I am simple which also implies for being poor. She said that I am very nice guy which also meant I am not capable of doing something great. Well her perfect murder was one heck of a skill. I think she is dead because she always thought of her as something extra ordinary, which is fine one should always believe, but the word belief comes with the word LIE in it. Her belief lied to her. Thinking of oneself highly is fine, but thinking of others as inferior can get you killed.

"And yes you must be wondering how could doctor miss the syringe wound, well 6 months back I suggested her to make a tattoo on her feet. I later suggested that red tattoo would look super sexy on her. It took me hours of pep talk; you know that sort of talk a man has to do for hours to make a woman do something for him. She made tattoo in red, I think that was the only time she ever listened to me. Thus, little mark of syringe in red was easily missed by doctors due to the tattoo."

"Story 2: Perseus & Medusa

You know my wife was a stage actress, you must have checked her history. A very mediocre actress, heaven knows why I fell for her. I felt terrible after couple of months of our marriage, she was an insane woman. But then I saw the silver lining when she told me a story of her fan, who went so crazy loving her that he landed himself into the asylum. He fell for her when he saw her pathetic play, she played role of the great "Aphrodite" and ever since then he worshipped her like an Aphrodite. This crazy guy was a big fan of Greek mythology & a sheer genius in maths. He had a great career in finance until he met my late beloved wife. As he was a very rich guy, my wife had a long affair with him but later my wife realized that he does not see her as she is, in fact for him she was still the Aphrodite: Greek goddess of love, beauty, pleasure. As per my wife, his expectation from their relation were reaching new heights every day, that no one can even imagine, if you know what I mean. Thus, eventually anxiety and obsession became his best friends and the guy ended up in the asylum punishing me unknowingly. Then my wife decided to find someone else; which was unfortunately ME. At first I believed the story, because she was quite convincing I think when any woman tells you a tale, beware of it. It is so convincing your heart goes out for them and you feel that they are not at all at fault. Only it takes years to realize it was all a big lie. That's where we men go wrong by believing their lies and we end up in their prison for lifetime.

So after 2 terrible years of my marriage, my magnificent wife gave me this sensational key to get rid of her, MADMAN!. She used to mention his name quite regularly & how awesome he was. It was her trick to hurt me so that I can push myself more & more and pamper her till eternity. That madman becomes the root cause of my unhappiness. But then I flipped my thinking. I thought maybe this Madman was a fine gentleman and actually my wife is so insane that she can drive anyone crazy. I felt from my gut that I should meet this guy and ask him what actually happened.

So I went to the asylum one day under a fake name, I met him and told him about my suffering and we both were on the same page. He turned out to be my brother in arms, he was a bit weird no doubt but my wife made him a psychopath for sure. I sobbed my sad story to him that how she was driving me crazy and torturing me emotionally every minute, I told him one day even I will join him in the asylum if nothing is done to her. He is the only one who can save me. I then insinuated that actually she is Medusa (An evil woman in Greek mythology) in the disguise of

Aphrodite who either turns men into nuts or kill them. I convinced him that he is the modern Perseus; The hero who beheaded Medusa. He is the only one who can save me. So I suggested him that he should blend in with world, pretend to be a mediocre just like them and then when he gets out of asylum; kill her. I gave him exact plan that after 6 months, he should come and kill her during the day time as I will be leaving the window open and he will not be caught as no one can relate to it. I told him I will not meet him again but I will leave the window open on my wife's birthday. I told him that if anything goes wrong with this plan I will inform him, but nothing went wrong for a year.

6 months later my words did the trick and heaven showed some grace on me. The mad man came home, killed my wife and I shed a tear of joy. He was a genius! he did a perfect murder he was not caught in camera, neither forced entries or exit nor struggle by victim. He was a god sent angel for me."

"Story 3: Her birthday Gift

We all have that fear in the childhood like someone is there in the dark or something is in the closet. We always used to open the closet with hesitation but with aging we lose that fear. We start opening closet without fear, that's where my wife went wrong. She should have opened the closet hesitantly. She would have been alive and I would have not been here sitting in front of you.

As you know it was her birthday when she was killed. We celebrated her birthday with lot of wine and weed. She fell asleep babbling how good & beautiful she is compared to all her friends and foes, I listened to it as usual, all the time hoping that this would be the last time I was listening to same old shit stories. Fact was she was indeed beautiful woman but with ugly mouth; she never spoke a good thing about anyone on the planet. She treated me as if she has done some sort of compromise or favour marrying me and it was my huge jackpot that I got married to her. Have you ever been through that? I felt really bad that I was never good enough for her though I was better in every possible way than her. Sex was always lousy and lately it was more sort of mercy sex to me, there was neither passion nor imagination in her. She had that melancholy air in her, which fascinated me first, we stupid men just can't resist a sad woman can we? we treat their problem as our problem and they keep on dumping their baggage on us and we carry it all our life. She became so self-absorbed that she could not even sense my mood lately, that's how terrible my life was. I had to be a joker all the time to keep her happy. So I decided to Man-up and end her problem, and her problem was herself. Until she dies she was never going to be a good factor to herself, me or any person in this beautiful world.

So before leaving for the office I planted the knife at the tip of a metal spring then I stick the spring box in the closet facing my lovely wife's dark heart. I placed a card on the table saying "Happy birthday love, your Gift is in the Closet & if you love me open with closed eyes" and after that I placed nice plastic mats surrounding the closet.

As expected, she was up around 2 pm even that was sometimes too early for her, at 2 pm I was in my office and praying that she should get killed. Those 2 hours from 2pm-4pm were hell for me and all I wished was that she should die by my death trap. I got no call from her till 4 I knew I was safe & she was dead. Never prayed in my life, but that drive home I prayed like it was my dying wish. What I prayed, came all true she was dead in front of closet but something went wrong at that time. I expected her to lie flat and I was stupid to think that knife would be left hanging by the closet but actually after getting stabbed she pulled the spring in shock thus entire box and spring got scattered around her. Fortunately, it helped me. It proved more realistic as she fell with the knife in her heart. All the blood was over her body and on plastic mat. Thus easy clean up. She was so drunk already she could hardly do anything about her state; she died in a systematic way. I must say luck was on my side this time, how stupid I was to think that knife would stab her; she will fall on the mat and knife would be left hanging by the closet. If she would have died like this my jig was up. Blood would be all over the closet and even if I wiped it blood would be easily traced by crime scene investigator. But fortune favours the brave. All her sins have brought this on her. Never mind.

So when I came home, I really had very less time to call police. Hardly 1 or 2 minute and after that 5 minutes max for them to arrive. So, all in all 7 minutes max. I came home wore my plastic overcoat which was made by me. I picked up the body placed it on the bed and called the police.

Then in the mean time I folded plastic mat, my coat, box and spring. Put them into bag and tossed them in the garbage located on the ground floor, if you remember I live on the second floor and if you look from the window which is located opposite of the main door. That window opens to rear side of the building and there is a garbage bin. I threw it, it was a perfect goal. I practiced for 2 months with garbage bag and my wife used to encourage me to hit the target. The only thing she ever encouraged me to do.

Police and garbage collectors arrived at same time. I knew I was a free man.

You came at scene full of vanity in that blue suit asking all sort of cliché question, just to add, you look first class fool in that blue suit.

"A perfect murder. Is it not Detective?"

Detective interrupted "You said your wife was a big time whiner, you are doing the same in front of me criticizing her in every possible way. No woman can be this bad and that suit looks great. All the girls in our department are crazy about it."

"One thing, I know about you for sure now, you have very less knowledge about women's psychology. Girls or women from the office lie almost 90% of the time to gain favours in future. You think I am whining, that's true, yes, but look at this way. You are the only person I can share this thing with. Now that my wife is dead I cannot say bad things about her to my friends or family. They will think for sure that I killed her, so you have to hear all this shit, it comes with the package" murderer smiled and moved to the 4th story.

"Story 4: Her Own Redemption

"Weed! A good of quality Marijuana and amateur level skill of convincing can make any one do anything. A little hallucination and induced fear, suggested solution can solve the entire problem. After 2 years of struggling marriage we both knew it was complete hell. We knew it was our personality's trait we both were never fit for marriage, I was indeed fed up of this woman and the word obnoxious was made only for her.

At midnight we started celebrating her birthday. After couple of wine glasses, we started our Bong session and this time I have brought most effective Marijuana straight from the base of Himalayas. It was very effective I must say. After we were high we always discussed negativity and ultra-level of pessimism. Only thing I knew about her was she held a Ph.D. in talking ill of others. So she was completely high by 5 am, I kept her up all night by pep talk and around 5 am I started to talk depressing things. Like how big failure we both were and we were no good to live our life.

And she wept and wept, accepted we messed up our life and we had no right to live. A life of failure is not worth living. After this sentence I started hypnotism or you can say some very efficient induced thinking suggesting suicide.

Before leaving for the office I left an audio recording, an old Cassette Player, beside the birthday card. She must have pressed play.

"Dear love, things have been terrible since we met and we both know this marriage is the greatest lie we ever told to ourselves. I knew all along that you were not in love with me, you still owed your heart to him. Last night you told me you are still in love with the guy in that Asylum. I was so shocked to hear that; that I made peace with myself by deciding to end my life. By the time you will hear this, I will be dead. But before ending my life I would really like to tell you something about yourself, which I could never say because of my love for you or may be because of my fear of losing you. But I know

now that I am losing you for sure, because I am done with you and your daily fiasco. I have given all the proof to police the way you tortured me mentally. My suicide will stick on your head and that will be your punishment for the life, you will spend your life in prison and that is worse than dying. So listen carefully why you will end up in prison.

"You are nothing but a self-loathing malicious woman, who was never happy herself nor even let people around you to be happy. Look around in your life, who is happy because of you? In fact, everyone is sad because of you for sure. Your parents who never gave up on you and you treated them like shit, your friends I am sorry are there any left? Your ugly teeth ate all. There was this genius fan of yours who is now in asylum. You think everything is about you and world is only concerned about your happiness. You always make sure that no one is happy around you. I should definitely be punished that I chose you, how a man of my character can ever fall for you. I do not regret dying but I do regret meeting you. You are the only reason for your and other's unhappiness. So do some favour and kill yourself rather than making your fellow prisoner unhappy as well. They say people who commit suicide go to hell, but I guess god will give you special place in heaven as you have done something good to humanity by killing yourself.

"You know this very well, your addiction will never end, alcohol and drugs are your soul sisters. You have lost your beauty long back, I lied and everyone lied to make you feel okay. But fact is you look terrible and irrecoverable, you cannot conceive anymore because of addictions & age, you are dead already. So, only thing that is left for you is to die gracefully, because in prison you will not last long because of your attitude."

I hope you die; Knife is in the closet. Hope you end all of your miseries, as I have.

She really did kill herself, detective, indeed stupid woman she was" finished the murderer.

"Coming to the last story will be your favourite, the answer you sought lies here. May I have Beer please? Watching your humbled face I feel a bit edgy, with the great show like this there should be some beers don't you think so?"

Detective went inside and brought a couple of beer and placed it in front of him with disgrace and said "You are a Whacko!"

"That is for sure I am" Quiz master smiled and continued to finale of puzzle

"Story 5: Detective's mystery solved

"All these days you were wondering how I got out of office premises without getting caught. My car was never caught leaving the Office premises and nor did I. I was not on the desk for sure between 2 to 4 Pm. I thought you would crack this simple mystery. It was simple detective, it was so simple, I wonder how you turned out to be such famous police detective with so many awards and just to remind you again, you look a first class fool in that blue suit.

There is guy who sits beside me, a nerd but addicted to Chinese food. Every Friday he goes for lunch at a Chinese restaurant located in the vicinity of my house. I suggested him once this restaurant and he really liked it. Little did I know that he would be this useful, that he would solve my life's problem, with a blink of an eye."

"So 1 Week before of my wife's murder I stole his car smart key" continued husband.

"But I checked every car! Every face" spoke the detective, "this is impossible."

"Patience lady!" snapped murderer "So stealing the key was easy as he was a careless man and his key was at the desk lying all the time. I Stole it. Car always comes with a set of 2 smart keys. As he lost his key, that very day I helped him to bring the duplicate key from his house. Now that I had the key, I checked that every day if it works or not. Key worked just fine."

"Then on the D Day, I parked the car on his usual spot thus he had to park at my space, where camera had no coverage. I remember your frustration when you came to my office and checked camera footage, blaming office security system for not keeping complete coverage. Do you know after your tantrum, all the office surveillance team was making fun of you and even they thought you look dumb in that blue suit. Do you wear that all the time?

Anyway coming back to your puzzles, by skipping camera, I got into the car by pressing the unlock button. You are aware of the new smart key just press unlock button and with couple of beeps all the doors are unlocked so I opened the backdoor of the car and settled in trunk and locked the car again. He went into that restaurant, I got myself out through the backdoor went into my house. Finished the only purpose of my life, killing her with my own hand, straight knife into her heart she hardly had any strength to feel her own death. I did one great job of killing an evil woman and

I am proud of it. And getting away with it, I think I am a sheer genius. After finishing the task, I got into the car and he escorted me back to the office."

"So that was it. I am done with all 5, what you think detective which story is true?" exhaled murderer.

"THINK THINK THINK!!!!! DETECTIVE

"I'll get some more beer and we can test your skillset. Remember, first you have to start by fake stories & why it is a lie and in the end you have to tell the real one. So first 4 lie and then 5th will be the truth so shall we begin."

Murderer returned with beers, detective did not appear quite sure which story was true and which were false, at one point all seemed fake to him and at some point all possible.

Murderer placed beers in front of him, ignoring the beer detective began.

"Story 4: Her own redemption.

Is sheer stupidity, I don't think a woman with such vanity will ever commit suicide not after listening to a pathetic loser like you. No doubt, she regretted marrying you; you are nothing but an ordinary man. She was the woman who almost tasted limelight but just like any other woman she was beautiful but not smart enough & ended up marrying a dumbass like you. It was a shame and I feel sorry for you, you must have been a nice gentleman before marrying her, but this type of women I have seen, they end up killing others but not themselves.

Well that was a psychological take on her character as much as you told me about her.

But logically, the knife was straight into her heart which cannot be the case when it is a suicide. In suicide, when a person stabs himself the knife never penetrates straight "90 degrees" it is always slant due to angle of hand. In your wife's case it was perpendicular not slant and that's how I knew it was not a suicide.

So a very bad story,"

"Story 2: Perseus & Medusa

I don't think this is possible, it is a well-constructed story though. But possibility of a guy getting himself out of asylum & waiting for 6 months to kill her. It is a bit too much expectation from the world and men are really not this patient. Plus, he loved that woman and her seduction was the reason he was in the asylum. He cannot kill her. Even if his heart was full of vengeance, then it would to take a very fit mind to do it. I mean, if this was the case he must have contacted her in recent months. I checked all the phone records and nothing was found regarding this man. I also checked the police record of your wife. There were only trivial cases regarding drugs but never complain of psychopath.

I think such person never existed. And you kept the window open all these day hoping someday he would come and kill her, I feel pity for you."

"Story 1: Blank syringe

It was a great plan or rather a story which almost got me thinking for a moment. Of course the autopsy guy never mentioned any mark on her feet and I do agree that he has been a bit lousy lately as he is going through a break up. Even if we consider that you inserted a blank syringe, let's say all you said happened perfectly. But one thing that made me think this story is baseless is because of the blood you poured. Autopsy can miss the syringe mark; they might miss conclude cause of death as heart attack. But it is impossible that my autopsy guy will not check the blood poured on her body.

We always check the blood around the body as well. The content of stored blood always is different. It was her blood; we checked it was fresh straight from heart. Medical science is not that stupid, this theory of blank syringe worked in 20th century but not in 21st.

And psychologically, you won't take that risk because injecting blank syringe might lead to heart attack. By luck if she survives heart attack or undergoes comma she would have been hospitalized. As you have to keep it a perfect murder so you yourself would take her to hospital. Doctors would have probably caught the reason behind her condition and your jig was up. Let's consider you say that luck was on your side in this murder. Doctor would probably treat her as normal heart attack and somehow even miss blank syringe. Let's say some how you pull this off but her medical condition was going to cost you a lot. I checked your financial condition you are broke; you cannot afford another blow to your finance.

Thus too many probabilities, luck factor and ifs & buts in this story…. So definitely a fake story. I highly appreciate your imagination though"

"Well things come down 2 stories." Gaining confidence and looking at empty beer bottles on the table detective went in and grabbed couple of beers, offered one to the murderer.

"Cheers!"

"Cheers!"

"Story: My mystery solved & Her Birthday gift(5 & 3)

"Well this is something baffling me, I mean both are really good, there is hardly any space for not being a perfect murder, but still I will crack it" continued the young confident detective.

"But I will justify both stories in parallel and then I will give you the final answer. One thing I must agree you have one heck of imagination or some real hatred towards your wife. Stupid Man and a Crazy Wife, women are not that bad as you think of them.

All right! What can I say, when it comes to these stories, they both are perfect but only one of these stories can be true right?"

Murderer smiled.

Ignoring his smile and not letting it affect his conclusion detective resumed his theory.

"Chances are good for both scenarios, your wife opening the closet, & you escaping the office through colleague's car, both scenarios are definitely possible".

"Wife opens the closets & yes the closet was little dark. It is possible she could not have seen it coming."

"In other story, you get in through the rear window. Ahh! you look fit. You can climb, for sure."

"You throw the evidence in the garbage bin possible in the closet Story.

"And you can also dispose gloves and plastic coat while exiting from the window in the 5th story."

"You make a Chinese Addict of that restaurant, even I have been there, they have offers on Friday lunch. So it is possible he can go there."

"What separates fake from real one I am wondering?"

"You were not seen by anyone while exiting out of the back door of the car quite possible and I checked the nearby street cameras but I am not sure if street cam covered the restaurant route so I can give you benefit of doubt for that."

"One thing that really bugs me in the closet story, I mean how come the knife has such a great accuracy that kills perfectly and I mean it is too much to the chance. But she was drugged and was not in senses plus as you said she fell with spring and knife in her hand, quite believable".

"I think you must have escaped from the driver seat of the car instead of backdoor, that why no one could catch you, as you crawled to front seat and then got out of car.

"Still equally balanced."

"This is not working but theory involves a stroke of luck in it, in fact all have luck factor, but these 2 has the lowest luck factor.

"No point in going logically, behind these 2 stories. I need to go psychologically."

"Let me think, give me last 2 mins to think"

Detective sat silent for 2 minutes.

"God! This was so simple…"

"You are a bloody coward and a loser."

I doubt you can go over and kill her by your hand. You are a henpeck husband for sure. I can still see you are in love with your late wife. You can only think of killing her by your own hand but I doubt you will be actually able to do it. So answer is

"Closet. Her Birthday gift"

"It fits perfectly Knife was quite perpendicular and you were quite right she would have fallen after getting stabbed with finger prints on the knife. But more importantly you did not have courage to kill her by your own hand so you needed this spring knife system."

"So this is it" proclaimed pompous detective.

"You're a coward, little stroke of luck, birthday and drugs in her body; this is the only story that can make sense and I remember we ignored the closet at crime scene no one dug deep in closet, even I threw just a short glance at it."

He smiled and then so did the murderer.

Then detective frowned.

Detective reached the envelope and hesitantly opened the envelope.

The digit was 2.

"No, this is highly impossible that was the lamest of all stories. Her EX-Crazy, Psychopath coming and killing her."

Murderer smiled "Yes, you are stupid, no need to rethink, you really bought that closet story. It is true and you are very right that I am a coward. How can I even think of taking a risk of planting knife into closet, just think, by any chance, knife missed her heart, I would have been dead in the next hour. You never had a terrible woman or wife in your life that's why you failed this case. The only wisdom I can share as a winning party, is a million-dollar suggestion."

"What?" asked the frustrated Detective.

"When it comes to woman always remember either they are Goddesses or Evil, there is no middle ground. They are best thing that can happen to you or the worst. Only way to judge a woman is by her action not by words, she might say she loves you but action always portrays a different picture."

"For me she was a goddess. I loved her and I still do despite what she has done with my life, but does not mean I was not allowed to kill her. You were right, I never had courage to kill my wife by my own hand as I was in love with her, but sometimes in life you have to kill a person because you love them."

"I will find that psychopath and prove the murder and both of you will end up in jail" grunted detective.

"Best of luck. You lose detective. Have a nice life & if possible stay away from evil women. World is full of them. All the characteristics, I mentioned in 5 stories regarding her were true. Remember those characteristics and tattoo them in your heart, it will save your life."

Murderer finished his remaining beer and departed.

Detective continued drinking....

THE END.

2

BLANK

Watching the city lights from the terrace of his rented apartment he smiled. It was only a matter of months' time or 2; he would be buying this apartment. He smirked on the second thought, he knew the woman who rejected him, shattered his heart into million pieces without even giving a single damn thought for his love to her, will now be his forever. *Now Who Wins! Girl. All your vanity will go down like a house of cards!*

He was happy that his greatest enemy TIME was his best friend now. He got the greatest gift any man can ever get. TIME!

The world was at his feet and he knew exactly what was coming. He knew that he was going to get each and everything he wanted in the coming year. All the rejection, humiliation, betrayals will be avenged now. Piece by piece, limb by limb, he was going to rip apart everyone who crossed his path. All his life women played with his heart like a game of dart, friends back stabbed him for the sake of love & money and for parents he never existed. His heart was not filled with hatred nor was he acting vindictive. He was just happy that for the first time since he was born things will go his way. These are his golden days. But he reminded himself after every thought that he was not going to hurt anyone; he wanted to keep his karma clean. His tremendous success will be answer to everyone who betrayed him.

Plan was ready, stage was set.

He went inside to open the bottle of Jack Daniels, something he craved since 2 years but he could hardly afford. He opened the bottle and smelled the aroma of upcoming success. He opened the gift which was given to him by his Ex, A fine whiskey glass just like his life. He filled a double of jack Daniel with 4 ice cubes. He went into living room, fortunately none of his roommates were home and he knew there won't be anyone until tomorrow. Laid back on his couch, he leaned to kiss his whiskey.

Bell Rang twice in quick succession, *this was not supposed to happen he thought*. He abandoned glass behind; with a dry throat he approached the uncanny.

He looked through the peephole, 2 gentlemen one dark and one fair dressed casually.

"Yes?" He questioned.

"Sir, please open the door" said the Dark guy.

"And who are you?"

"We will explain, let us in" said fair guy.

"Not until you tell me know who you guys are."

"Let us in sir, we mean no harm; there is some important thing you need to know."

He timidly opened the door. Guys came in and calmly settled on the sofa.

"Please sit, Sir we need to ask you few question."

"Is everyone alive and well, there is no Bad news right?"

"Fortunately, No" replied fair guy.

"Thank god! I thought something went wrong" He said.

Ignoring his remark, the fair guy asked "What happened with you in last 2 days?"

"What?"

"We already know what happened, we want to know HOW it happened" added fair guy.

"What are you talking about? Nothing happened everything is usual" he lied.

"We can see bottle of Jack Daniels, well seems like someone is celebrating on a weekday with bottle of costly whiskey, there must be some great reason for celebration."

"Well let me put this in a very simple way" added dark guy. "We deal in this thing, what happened to you is not good for your health and you can be in a grave danger."

"What thing?"

"The thing that happened to you, it is not a first time we are dealing with and if you do not cooperate ...." he finished by placing silenced revolver.

"So I suggest you should start talking. Tell me what you saw in detail and we will promise to take care of you."

Looking at the revolver with terror in his heart he began narrating events took place in last 2 days.

"48 hours earlier

I lost everything, all money I saved & invested in a friend's scheme which turned out to be a big sham and he got away with all of my money. The stock in which I invested hit rock bottom and I was bankrupt in a single day. With the remaining money I bought a diamond ring for my girlfriend & proposed her but she refused saying she has someone else on her mind and requested not to see her again. I went home got heavily drunk with my roommate. I took leave from the office next day as I was too hungover. But my roommate insisted on going to office despite of heavy dose of alcohol and crashed to death. He was the only friend I had.

So in a single day, I lost all of my money, love and my best friend & confidence. My Job was not interesting. I was doing it so that I can save some money, invest it and create my own business empire but now I was broke. I came home after my roommate death and got drunk again. This time I drank myself to death. I don't remember much but I do remember jumping off my balcony from the 7th floor. Air!! When it touches your face it is like angels kissing you, before impact I regretted only one thing, I should I have jumped from the Top floor instead of 7th. I touched ground to wake up in my bed.

I was soaked, that nightmare left me completely drained. I could not get up for few minutes, then somehow gathering all my wit, I thanked god that I am alive and my life is not that bad.

After couple of bottles of water, I was in my senses; I found my apartment quite fresh as if it was newly painted. My roommate was still sleeping, I wondered why he was still asleep. It was 9 am and he was supposed to be in office. I woke him up and asked him to move on with his duty; he simply replied "Buzz off." I laughed, got ready and left my apartment. But the nightmare was still haunting me. I was waiting for the lift, the lift door opened and a beautiful girl passed by me, I knew I have seen her before, it was one of those faces one can never forget, never mind.

I got into my car and I drove through the town. It looked quite new to me in a way, traffic was less. It was less humid. I reached office, parked my car and went into the lobby for the security check. I saw the old Security guard.

"Oh! You are back, how are you?" I asked with a smile.

"Back? When did I leave?" he asked surprisingly.

"No, you left the job right? You wanted to take care of your family business."

"No Sir, I am still here, I am not going anywhere."

"Okay.." I said thinking something is wrong with him.

So I entered into the office, well I am an employee of a company that produces series of flop games and they still think of themselves as giant. So after entering I saw, all the colleagues were sticking posters of all the old gaming titles which are already been released.

So I asked one of my obnoxious colleague "Why are we again sticking posters of the old game titles instead of the upcoming ones?"

My colleague passed a cold stare at me and replied "How much did you have last night"

"GOD! I am not a drunkard."

"Boss, is looking for you and seems like he got usual whipping from his wife"

"Damn!"

I entered casually into the lion's den, "So what's up, when is the next project coming up? It is been long time since I am on the bench? And why are we sticking the posters of the game which we have already released?

He too passed a Cold stare at me, closed his laptop and asked me to take a sit.

"Cold day, it is" I said.

"How much you had last night, at least 1 litre of whiskey I guess?"

"No, what is wrong with everyone today, I am not drunk."

"We agreed yesterday that we will be in office at 7 am instead of 10, as we have a client visit. Here you are the so called People Person of our great company late by 3 hours. Hope you are at least ready with presentation?"

"No, which client?" I asked bluntly.

"**MICROSOFT**, does that name make any sense to you, you know Microsoft right? Though they just make billions of dollars every year..."

"They are coming again?" I interrupted.

"What you mean by again?"

"I mean last time they visited they rejected us because of our poor infrastructure."

"How do you know that, who told you this?"

"Everyone knows about it."

"How? Damn! Our CEO must have blurted out over the drinks, sometimes I wonder if he is a CEO or a drunkard BBC correspondent of our company."

"Anyway, are you ready with the presentation?"

"No, you never said I have to."

"I did & I also sent you a mail"

"No, I don't think so" I replied timidly.

Check your mailbox or here it is, he opened his laptop and showcased the mail to me

"See, there it is, do you want me to read it aloud to you?"

"No, I can see it but we did it before."

"When?"

"Last year."

"Were you in that team?"

"Yes, you added me."

"What? I don't remember, I should quit drinking it is affecting my memory. Anyway, create a presentation. I really don't have time for memory games"

I went to my desk, opened my laptop and checked my mailbox. Nothing normal birthday mail by HR, HR, god! They must find some better things to do rather than forwarding birthday, Christmas, Easter mail's all the time. Next thing I searched was last year's presentation for the Microsoft, I couldn't find it. Then I checked my hard drive but no luck. I asked my colleague if he has that presentation, well answer was cold stare. I went to my boss and asked if he still has presentation from the last time, his reply was simple "Be original."

Something was wrong I could feel it, something was definitely wrong. Then it dawned on me that maybe everyone is messing with me. Because currently we were having no work and it was sort of a prank week going on. Anyway, I knew what presentation I have to create, just copying pasting stuff from here and there, 20min and the presentation was done. I mailed it to my boss.

"I am smart, as you guys already know" he scorned at the 2 guys sitting on his Couch, You guys do not have sense of humour; I am the one in threat here, anyway, so coming back to my story."

Throwing glance at his whiskey, which now had no ice, he continued his story.

"Boss appreciated my presentation. He was dumb enough not to figure out that it was a straight rip off from my previous presentation. 1 pm and to my surprise the Microsoft did show up. Since the entry of Microsoft guys, I knew my life has gone haywire.

He interrupted the story and asked the 2 guys sitting at his couch "Have you ever had that feeling when you know everything has actually happened all you need is an official proof?" he tried to make his story a bit interactive with his new company but he was talking to the wall.

He continued his story.

"I dealt with the client and all along I had Déjà vu for straight 4 hours. By the end of the day I started to sync with my déjà vu and started to predict the next thing and next word they were going to utter. It was not calculation; I Just knew it. Somewhere in the corner of my mind I knew what has actually happened. I knew but I was in denial, I needed proof.

Client departed. I knew, we were not going to get them.

I went to my desk, opened my laptop and I was staring blankly at my screen. I could not figure out what was happening. Office time was over and I checked time at the bottom right corner of my laptop screen.

It was 6 pm 20 Aug.

Half hour to leave the office I thought but then it clicked me, something was wrong with time & date and I checked it again; something indeed terribly was wrong with my time and date. I checked the time again.

It was 6 Pm 20 Aug 2014. I was shocked.

I asked date & time to my colleague he replied 20 Aug 2014. I checked every one's laptop and mobile date was 20 Aug 2014. I went to the reception to check today newspaper date was 20 Aug 2014. This can't be for real I thought.

He looked at his 2 audience. Both held their poker face intact. No eyebrows raised whatsoever.

"Have you ever felt that moment, when you know absolutely everything has changed, nothing is ever the same again. But this time it is in your favour. You can feel it in your every breath that finally you are going to win. With years of struggle finally something has happened in your favour. Have you ever heard that song by Phil Collins 'in the air tonight'? I guess no, but yes do listen to it. You will thank me."

Ignoring his poor audience. He resumed his story.

"But I needed concrete proof that what has happened to me is not a prank. My emotion and logic both were in denial."

"Then?" asked the fair guy first time entering into the story.

"There is one strange thing on the planet, we men call it women. I knew, she was the only way I can confirm it. We men are so stupid when it comes to women. All Roads lead to Women, not Rome I would rather say" he laughed and expected some reaction from his audience but he sighed and continued.

"So I went to my music academy where I expected her to wait outside for me at 7pm. she was never late, but she was not there this time. So I barged into my class, the tutor asked me who I was and what I was doing there and straightway refrained from showing me any sign of familiarity, but I was busy searching her, I saw her and I waved at her, she completely ignored me, as if she saw me for the first time.

I checked with receptionist. I was not enrolled in the music academy. Now my heart confirmed the phenomenon that has occurred to me is true because the girl did not recognize me. My Heart accepted this dramatic change but logic was still unconvinced.

I left music academy. I walked along the street asked strangers todays date, they all replied 20 Aug 2014. My happiness knew no bounds now.

"One last test I had to take, because friends, love, colleague can prank you sometimes even stranger can prank if they were place strategically, but government won't play prank, So I went to One tree hill"

"You know that place right?" he asked his audience

"No we do not." They replied in sync.

"Okay, so there is a small hill with one tree on it, north from here just few miles away. Once you climb that little hill you can see the city and suburbs quite distinctly and I could see there was still no hanging bridge across the river. The old bridge was still active and present.

"The Over Bridge was not constructed yet. That moment I knew I was a rich man. Now let's see, my colleague can fool me, music academy and woman I love can trick me, even the newspaper in my house, company can be a lie. Let all be a big Lie. But the prank cannot be this grand that they would demolish over bridge."

"What's this all has to do with Over bridge" asked fair guy.

"Tell me today's date?" He asked him.

"21 Aug 2014."

"Exactly, the bridge will be constructed by 21 Aug 2015."

"I was on the hill all night. I planned my each and every move for coming year, this time I had edge against world. I was one year ahead of everyone I knew what will be coming. I came home this morning checked newspaper checked stocks, everywhere it was 2014 instead of 2015. I knew my roommate will be going out of town. I slept whole day, woke up in the eve to complete my planning. Got a bottle of JD and then you guys show up. That's what happened to me. That's what I know. I guess my life will be better now. And now I realize that I will commit suicide on the night of the 20 Aug 2015, and I will not let it happen."

"Sir, you need to come with us" added the fair guy

"Why? It is not my fault, that I woke up and I am in 2014 instead of 2015. Maybe I had premonition who knows"

"Well, it is hard to explain for us as we are not the scientist who has all the answers. But we can assure you that you will get all the answers once you come with us."

"I don't want to be a god or something, I just want to fix my life and be successful."

"That no one can predict, power is crazy thing sir, which can even make god go crazy and you are just a human" remarked dark guy.

"I don't have power to change the course of future. Best I can possibly do is earn some money and get my love. That's it. 1 house 1 car and some publicity, fame and I can go on" he said mockingly.

"But your action, can stir changes in others' lives which can start a chain reaction or worst you can go mad by yourself or even bored and take lethal step as you know what is going to happen."

"I am sure I won't go mad; things will be just fine. I will win and I promise you I will not harm anyone. In fact, you can keep your men around me".

"Sir, we insist you to come with us."

"Where?"

"That you will know."

"What if I deny?"

Dark guy looked at the revolver.

"What? how can you do that."

"You know too much, we cannot let you Intervene the natural course of nature, Sorry"

"I promise you, I will not do any harm. I swear I will not do anything new. I know you guys might take me to lab and study my brain, but tell me what wrong have I done. Was it my fault, that this phenomenon occurred to me?"

"We never said we will kill you, we need your help in fact. And if you can't help us then, yes, we have to kill you."

"So what will you do to me? Will I come back?"

"We don't know."

"So this is it, my life is over you mean to say? All of my life I struggled, I fought, thought and thought, how I can make my life matter. Never betrayed anyone nor messed with anyone. Then finally my brain and my thinking found a way to turnaround my life. You guys barge in and tell me I am done. When world was unfair to me you did not show up that time. I know I am talking to the wall; you guys are going to take me anyway. But let me assure you one thing, this will not end well for you as well."

They smiled.

"But I have a wish. Let me have my last drink."

Fair guy looked at dark guy, got his approval.

He took out a new glass. He filled double with lot of ice. Staring at the glass, he smiled finally it is all over for him no more love shit, Money madness, Power persuasion, just nothing. He thought of calling to say goodbye to his loved one's but then refrained.

He settled on the couch. The guys were staring with their dead eyes.

"Would you like to have a drink?"

Anticipating the answer to his question, "Then would you please stand outside my door, I don't want to have my last drink looking into the eyes of my death"

"We will be waiting outside, if you do not show up in 10 min, we will drag you out or kill…"

"I know, I know. Now please leave this house, I will join the party very soon" He said.

They left. He kissed whiskey; little while ago it was supposed to be his success drink and now his last.

Thinking of his situation he laughed loudly for almost a min.

"Funny it is, funny it is" he said it to himself. He always used to say that when he loose. And he will never know what he might say after winning in life.

He stared into the ceiling feeling the warmth of the whiskey going through his chest the only thing he can cherish. His entire life flashed in front of him. Then he realized he has learned so much in his life that if he survives this he would rule the world. He didn't need this future vision to win. He was happy because his failure had more grace than other people's success.

A Tear rolled out of his eyes for the first time in his life. With a Smile on his face he gulped his last sip of whiskey.

Let's face it! He thought jumping out of balcony might not work this time or running or calling police for help in such short span will not be of any use.

He stood, "Game On!" he said and slammed the glass on the wall, followed by the whisky bottle!

They rushed in.

"Easy, ladies" he said

"Enough, let's go!" commanded the dark guy.

He led the way out of the apartment followed by his new body guards. He pressed the lift button. He wished that beautiful woman would pass by him again, at least some solace before departure.

The lift door opened to an empty space.

"After you", said the fair guy.

He entered inside followed by his shadows.

Lift door closed, he took a deep breath and they closed his eyes.

Aftermath

Video went Viral & victim became overnight star, CCTV footage of 3 men entering into a lift at the 7th floor which stops straight at -1 floor but no one leaves the lift, thus making three men disappear into the lift. The video swept entire world, in 5 days it had billion views on You tube.

After missing report was filed by the victim's parents, a thorough investigation was carried by police but they couldn't find a single clue related to the Victim's disappearance. The CCTV Footage was tested in the best lab but it was cleared of any tampering.

As per police chief, "It is quite unfortunate that his disappearance is a big mystery and we still could not find a breakthrough, we are trying our best to find him. And the other 2 guys who abducted him."

Victim's friends and family used his story to reap profit by interviewing on every possible news channel.

Lot of conspiracy theories were evolved. Dr. Campbell, come to a theory and according to him government or unknown forces are behind this miraculous incident. "This has been happening since a long time, there are few special ones on the planet who disappear without a trace. We can do nothing about it. The only conclusion I can make is that all these personalities had different set of brain. They see things which no one could see. They probably are locked somewhere but don't know where."

Epilogue

Somewhere…

"So as per our deal you are now famous and everyone is talking about you, So now it's time to keep your part of deal and tell us what's coming this year" asked their chief.

"But how did you find me?" Victim questioned.

"It is very easy actually; we use infrared satellite imagery or thermographic satellite imagery concept. We sort of keep the temperature watch on the humans, suppose if the temperature of the human goes beyond normal which is Hyperthermia. Our system displays only those individual which hit more than 45 degrees Celsius. Though death is certain at 45, your temperature was 50 degrees that night which was too much to take for a human body. In your case you did not travel back in time, which you probably might have felt at some time but you were smart enough to figure out it was premonition; it was advanced level premonition in simple language. That night in your dream, your brain went through unusual pattern and this pattern led to entire vision of future. Your calculation was so perfect & Vivid that you thought you are in 2015 instead of 2014. In a way you believed it was 2015 but you were in 2014. That's why security couldn't understand you, Microsoft showed up, your love did not recognize you and you know the rest. You joined the music academy because of her. You knew her before meeting her in the music academy, probably has seen her somewhere. You could predict because you were naturally very good at probability and prediction, no wonder you were good in betting all your life, it's a shame you never took betting seriously. Special minds are always under confident, which you were all your life. Lack of confidence was your failure factor.

"Are you my Dad?"

Chief smiled.

"So can we stop discussing my failure and comeback to what happened that night?" He added disdainfully.

"We human subconsciously always calculate, plan or try to predict future. Like for example I will do this in the afternoon or that in the evening or tomorrow or the weekend. We do this daily. When it comes to small plans we can predict almost 80% correctly. In the same way we also try to calculate the future which only 20% of the time is correct. But calculating future in dream is something very different, only special minds can do it which you did."

"All right. If I understand it correctly, It is a machine which locates people who run through extreme unusual energy, then you catch those people and bring them here in this lab and try to know what is going to happen in future, so that you can make money out of it. Oh! Sorry, you sugar coated it by saying you are trying to understand future so that you can make it better"

"Yes, you can draw your own conclusion" said Chief.

"But how did you know, I saw the future?"

"We did not know that, we played bluff when we said we know this "THING" and you blurted out the entire story, it took us 24 hours to find you. Our machine can point to only geographical location not exact person, so we did some investigation with security guard of your building and he said you were the most unusual person in the building and we found you"

Victim smiled. "Bravo! So you want to know what's next? in Syria war or you want to know what Julian Assange is going to leak or do you want to know Oil war or the economy of the world?"

"All of it" smiled the proud Chief.

"So, your guys told me while abducting me, that I might change the course of the future. Yes, well you are right, telling you would definitely change the course of future"

"What do you mean?"

"You know what happened that night? What have I actually seen? Well note this down, Next year is going to be very peaceful and things are going to be just fine, as per my vision. Telling you things which I have actually seen might change the entire course of the future. I think I will be the one, who will have the last laugh now. And if you still did not get what I just said, let me tell you in very simple words

"I AM NOT GOING TO TELL YOU."

Silence spread across the lab.

"So Yes, You can use your revolver now. I am done."

BLANK....

THE END

3

FOLLOWING...

WAR always leaves you empty handed and if you lose, will leave you shattered. It's a terrible feeling, especially when you are defeated by someone way more inferior. It is a Nail in your heart which pokes you every time it beats. For a defeat like this there is no physiological recovery. You realize that you have to live with it all your life, like a soul stuck in purgatory.

. . .

My days in London were almost over, only 25 days left for my return to homeland. I was excited, ecstatic and couldn't wait to see my loved ones. Monday morning, I had a beautiful dream. I was in a heavenly place with all of my loved ones. It was dawn, I was up but didn't feel like opening my eyes to the daily mundane tasks. Eventually, alarm went off. I was supposed to open my eyes with a smile on my face but I opened my eyes to a nightmare.

It was there on my chest and staring right into my eyes. My heart stopped, I jolted sideways, hitting my head on lamp followed by drawer's edge. I was dreaming again but this time it was all dark. I heard some faint noise, I couldn't recognise it first, but it was my alarm. I opened my eyes slowly to my carpet. How the hell did I sleep on the floor? I wondered, then it struck me what had just happened. My head was hurting like hell and I was still scared. Gathering all the courage I raised my head, SHE was still there staring at me, making my bed her kingdom. She smiled mockingly at me, and then went away from the balcony door. What the hell? Was she just waiting for me to give me a final glance? I checked my phone I was knocked out for almost 30mins.

With a swelling on my forehead, I went to the office. Everyone laughed at my story. Initially, I decided to tell them I got hit in the bar to sound cool, but ended up telling the truth. Yes, I told them the truth which generally I don't. I forgot about the entire incidence by next day.

Days went by and the sunny Saturday afternoon finally arrived. Time for that special nap, at this time even Gods are asleep, I am sure of that. After a hearty English breakfast in brunch I lay on my sofa, feeling great about my life. A dozens of beer in the refrigerator, couple of new game titles for my PS3 (both ps3 and game title I got for free from a friend) what more can a man ask for? I turned off my phone, now no whats app, no calls, just absolutely nothing. I closed my eyes and I was in the wonderland. I was lucid dreaming of Goa. I was on the beach with my beloved beer.

I heard some consistent tapping noise. I thought the noise was in my dream but that was not the case. First, I thought it was water from the tap then the intensity of tapping noise increased rapidly. I was so bored to open my eyes, but I had to sort it out. I wanted to have my beer peacefully in Goa. Unwillingly I opened my eyes. No prizes for guessing, there was that witch walking on my floor as if it belonged to her. I would be lying if I say she didn't startle me but this time I improvised by not falling off the couch. Well, TIME FOR VENGENCE.

I stood up on couch and jumped behind the witch. She responded calmly by moving ahead, as if I have done nothing special. I was never being taken so lightly in my life. I shooed her but that witch barely moved, *I mean come on!!*. Then I realised, I have actually cornered her as balcony door was half closed. Witch knew how to get in but not out, how dumb. *That was the last time I called it dumb.*

So, I slowly went around she was between couch and TV, spotting my every move like a Sniper. Timidly, I opened the balcony door wide open. I came back around again and shooed her she hardly budged; *seriously?* how the hell someone can be this stubborn. I decided to get aggressive. I went into the other room and brought my belt. Don't worry I am not one of those morons who hurts others. So I flung one end of the belt near to her, she moved swiftly towards the door, Inches before the door she stopped and turned around. Staring at me with all fear in her eyes, which I actually misjudged at that time, it was not the fear but warning in her eyes saying "Not a step more!" Yeah I am poor at reading body languages and now I am poor at reading body language of a witch as well, I guess that's why I am unmarried.

I took a step forward, waved my belt in front of her. she was not moving. What is wrong with this thing? So I decided to slam the belt before her and unknowingly I became her nemesis. It did hit that witch and it flew away right out of the balcony door, I was so proud of myself, I was a bit harsh but it was an honest mistake. I came out to my balcony with a belt on my shoulder like a bandit. There were my neighbours sipping beer, their balcony was vertically opposite of mine which belonged to Mr Christian & his girlfriend from Denmark.

"hahaha, I saw her going in your house and was waiting for you to come out, it took you quite a while to get her out" shouted Christian.

"Did you hurt that poor thing?" asked his girlfriend, thinking I am a moron who would do such stuff. I didn't know her name so her name is girlfriend in this story; So remember her name is girlfriend and remember she is very important, just kidding nothing as such.

"No No No" I said "I just used it to scare her away."

"We were sitting here and enjoying the show, You did good" said Mr Christian.

"Yeah, I didn't know how it got inside through such a small opening of balcony door" I replied.

"No, she got in through that balcony" He pointed to the balcony of my bedroom which also faces north. I turned around and that witch was there standing calmly in the balcony. I rushed to my other bedroom to close the door so that witch shall not come in.

I reached the balcony door and I pushed it hard, I was halfway closing the door then something hit me very hard right in the middle of my fore head. I was numb for few seconds couldn't understand, what has just happened. Somehow I closed the door. The witch was still in the balcony. Then something hit on the glass door, my neighbour was firing, it was this plastic golden spherical bullet that came out of his airgun hit me few seconds back. Now this man is called moron! Not me. But that witch won't believe me. I was the villain in her life not that imbecile hunter, who emptied almost 40 bullets but couldn't hit one to her. After watching such a disgraceful performance of the hunter, the witch went away.

Finally, after running out of all bullets, he shouted, "You Ok?"

"Yeah" I replied, what was I supposed to say or complain about? Should I scream that he was a terrible shooter, that he couldn't even shoot an easy target, or should I appreciate him for hitting the bull's eye which was my forehead. Saturday afternoon was completely ruined. The time was 5 pm. I thought of having my beer but I was too pissed off. I needed something heavy for my soul. So I invited 2 guest's MR Jack Daniel's and Miss Diet coke. Party began, 1 glass after another, music, daydreaming, lost thoughts and the sun finally went down at 9 pm, that's all I remember. Next morning, I woke up and saw the empty bottle of whiskey and a large pizza box. God! I don't remember finishing that pizza and Half of JD. This is unfair I don't remember eating pizza, so I ordered again for the afternoon.

Monday morning, the moment I entered my office, my Colleague asked, "What's the spot on your fore head?" Embarrassingly, I told her entire story over the coffee machine and she kicked off her Monday morning by laughing and mocking me. Anyway, at least it made some one laugh.

I started my work, but my head was into the witch, so I opened Google and typed.

How to get rid of **PIGEON**…. UK, word UK was auto suggested.

I smiled, I was not the only one in UK with this problem. So I surfed from one website after another but all solutions were going to cost me money. Physical bird deterrent, Chemical deterrents, Sonic bird deterrents, Ultrasonic devices, these websites were serious it's like they have declared war against pigeon. They sounded more outraged than me; some website indirectly hinted 'JUST KILL IT'. God! World is full of morons unlike me. Anyway, I got number of bird control and I called them. My Colleague who sits beside was smiling when I called, she was all set for movie. I could see that invisible popcorn in her hand and enjoying my movie.

Call got connected. "Bird control, how can I help?"

"Well, I have pigeon problem and I need your help."

"Do you mean Pieeegooon" she replied in typical English accent.

"Yeah" I replied.

"How many are they and how are they troubling you."

"It's just one pigeon, coming into my house regularly and messing around."

"Oh! Just 1 Pieeegoooon?"

"Yeah."

"Does it have a TAG on it?"

"Taaaag?" I asked.

"Well there are 2 types of pigeons, one is wild and other one is owned. So next time you see that pigeon if it has tag on its leg, it belongs to someone. Note the tag number and there is a website where you can report but remember you must capture it first, yeah?"

"Catch it?"

"Yes, there is website you can check the details on it."

So I jotted down the website called homingpigeon.co.uk

"And what if it does not have tag on it? what am I supposed to do then?"

"Well, if it is just one pigeon you should install some trap to catch it and then deliver to nearby bird agency or you can install some nets to stop pigeon from entering. You can find these traps and nets on amazon and Ebay."

"And if there are too many pigeons then we can send some expert to help you out, but it is going to cost you."

"No, it's Ok I am not going to pay for 1 stupid pigeon" I laughed.

"That's what they all say" She laughed. That was definitely an evil laughter, she underestimated me.

"Okay, I will check the tag first, thank you so much."

I hung up the phone, my colleague was still smiling

"Are you going to pay for cute pigeon" she asked.

"I am not gonna pay for that filthy pigeon" I replied wryly.

"Pigeons are so cute, how can you call them filthy?" she complained.

"Girls like anything, what's there to like about pigeon, it's just a pigeon a stupid filthy pigeon."

"You won't understand the beauty of nature."

"Okay, if I catch it I will gift it you." I tried to close the argument.

"Excellent, but I bet you won't catch it, it's not your cup of tea" She continued.

"Will see."

So changing the topic, I asked "Do we have any work today? or it's just like any other day of doing nothing."

"I thought you would never ask, life is not all about that pigeon" she replied.

"Okay, so we do have some work finally, great!"

"No work to do today as well, enjoy your daydreaming of pigeon" she laughed. *Damn! She is really enjoying my show.*

So turning my face to my laptop, I checked the website it clearly mentioned:

PLEASE NOTE:- **DO NOT** report pigeons that are not in your possession. Owners cannot arrange to collect pigeons that are roaming or flying around your home or garden. You must catch the pigeon first.

"Excellent" I thought. Now I have to catch the bloody pigeon by hand or install the stuff worth at least 25 Pound. I am not going to touch that filthy thing; honestly I am scared to touch it. I did catch snakes, spiders and even a rat they were never filthy to me. But pigeons are definitely awfully filthy.

So after another day of doing nothing in office, I returned home. I was waiting for the pigeon. I was desperate to know if it has a tag on it. Anxiety was at its peak, similar to a man waiting for his first date or his wife's delivery. I wanted this nightmare to get over as soon as possible. Anxiety is the worst feeling. It never lets you live, plus it fires up all the negative emotion to top level.

Now 3 days passed but the pigeon didn't show up. I always knew when you are really desperate about something it will never show up at the right moment it will usually come when you have lost all the interest in it. It is like result of your exam, call / text from someone you love, or it's like flight back to home which never arrives on time.

Finally, when I almost gave up hopes for that witch, on the Friday eve she showed up on the balcony railing. First I thought not to engage in this mission and it will go away. So I continued with my PS3. It started raining quite heavily and I could see the witch shivering with cold. I said "Suffer you Witch, suffer!" But men are emotionally weak no matter what they say. They are weaker, especially if they have alcohol in them; yes there are few exceptions like my neighbour, who maybe by now loading his gun. Finally, I thought to show some mercy and let the bird in, planned to throw her out once the rain is over. So I opened my balcony door. But the witch was not coming in. So I went into the kitchen to make her feel more secure. She got in.

I felt good and I even threw some bread crumbs, witch loved it. GOD! You there??, add some extra point in my karma or luck account I did good. I was watching her and she was watching the rain. It stopped raining, so time to go lady! I again tried the old flop way of Shooing, it didn't work. So time to bring out my belt only this time I will be more care full, I made her move a bit but failed. What was I supposed to do I can't afford to be a moron again. So this time I took mop to poke it.

So I poked, she took a flight and landed on the teapoy. Mom always used to say "don't keep money around" I never paid heed until today. The bird jumped a little to reach 20 £ note and began poking it. Hostage situation! I gave away my mop and said "Easy, easy we can talk, no one needs to get hurt, it is between you and me, 20 £ has nothing to do with it" ignoring me she continued poking. But Queens Face on the note was not something she can drill into. Bird was trying desperately but couldn't poke through it. I smiled "you lose, and queen is not something to poke around". Next second something unimaginable happened. As the poking failed she got her beak on the edge of the note and locked it hard. So now table is turned, there can be abduction of my note. I immediately picked up my mop and decided to poke the witch headstrong. I poked slowly, but no use someone flew away out of balcony door with my 20£ note, I paced after it till the balcony but it was already sky high. Pigeon owes me 20£. Now this is personal. I was wild with rage. The neighbours were there, they saw the whole show again.

"HAHAHA" laughed Christian again. "You should not have let it in. Money gone!! Boy."

He had his orange air gun in his hand. "Here take this gun, have it and get rid of it once and for all."

His girlfriend snapped "No!... are you crazy don't give the gun to him it belongs to my son."

"Love, we have a bigger purpose, he needs to have it" consoled Christian. He threw the gun towards me as the balcony was just 6 meters away. I caught it.

"Time to pick up weapons" I said to myself. I removed the magazine of the gun it was fully loaded with at least 20 bullets. Loaded the magazine thanked him and promised to return him once I am done.

Next morning, I woke up and again I couldn't remember when I ate pizza, I ordered it again. And then I saw the gun, what was I thinking yesterday "kill a bird" am I moron? NO I am not going to keep the gun, this is crazy. So I went to my neighbour to return the gun, but they were not at home. They left town last night.

Sunday morning hangovers are the worst; you simply are not in a position to do anything. Somehow I gathered my wits, did the laundry and cleaned up. In the eve I decided to take a stroll, I really needed some time to think about life, which was this pigeon at this point. During my stroll on the high street, I came across a tarot card reader. I never visited one, I really wanted to play with their mind. Once I researched a lot about the hot and cold reading and I knew it like the back of my hand. 20 pound for the session, I must enter. I really wanted to piss off someone, so its tarot card reader's turn today.

I went inside, all the things that I expected were there, gothic pictures, antiques and the dark curtains.

I heard the voice, "come on in lad." The eloquent voice was of a lady around 40 years of age. Pushing away the red dark curtain, I faced her.

She was sitting on the leather chair behind table with a stack of cards, she looked 60 not 40. She had a magnificent aura; she seemed quite energetic & lively. She had more energy and enthusiasm compared to an any 30-year-old woman. Honestly, I was impressed by her Appearance, voice and body language. *Don't get impress you fool, you are here only to spend 20 pound, drive her mad, remember hot and cold reading lesson and play her game against her.*

"Hi" I said.

"You have travelled far my boy, you have seen the seven seas, but still you are seeking something, the answer to everything" she foretold.

I smiled "Everyone is looking for an answer, tell me what answer I am seeking. And by the way, I have not travelled 7 seas; I am just new in UK."

"No, son almost year now I can see in your face you are weary single traveller."

Impressive, she must have seen me many times, in this area, that's their job, also 7 seas was fluke shot so no need to get all excited and impressed.

Sitting in the haunted room I said. "This can be a good bar, interiors are really different" *all the worlds weirdo would love to come and have drink here, I thought.*

She laughed "Thanks, this is actually my drinking place" and winked.

Fancily, she branched out all the tarot cards in front of me. "Pick 3" she asked

I hesitantly put my finger on a random card.

She flipped the first card, looked into my eyes and smiled; *my wife should be this graceful when she is 60.*

I chose second card. She flipped the second card and looked into the ceiling, I had no choice but to look at ceiling there was absolutely nothing, heaven knows what that women saw, this is a madhouse for sure.

I chose 3rd card. She flipped the 3rd card she didn't look at me neither nor at ceiling but she got up and went behind the black curtains.

Meanwhile, I was happy. This woman was really different she had her own play which was different from what I have read or saw on the T.V.

She came back with a huge book and placed it on the table.

"What is this?" I asked.

"Reference from the past, there was a girl if I remember it correctly; she was the only person who selected combination of these 3 cards, and now it's you." She opened book flipped the pages in bunch and finally reached her desired page.

"Yes, I was right same case. Look all 3 cards just like you."

I checked, her name was Nancy and date of her visiting this madhouse was my date of birth which was interesting. So some 25 years back when I was born, a woman came in here and chose exact 3 cards just like me, I tried to conceal my surprise.

"So what happened to her?" I asked.

"I don't know she was the only case for which I couldn't do anything nor say anything. She never came back, she was a traveller just like you. As I remember she had seen the world, she had achieved all the things she wanted, but something was missing, that question she asked me "what is missing?" and I had no answer to that."

"What brings you here?" she asked.

Now looking at her seriousness, I cannot answer *Pigeon*.

One should never be a good liar which I was, unfortunately. But I only lie to make anyone feel good about them. I guess that's what all liar's say.

So I had to lie. I took a deep breath (*that's where I failed and that's where she caught my intention of coming there, never take a deep breath before lying at least not in front of experts like this woman. These fortune-tellers are specialised in reading body language*), "I don't know, I just came in, no specific reason I felt lost in my life. But this is interesting; the woman came on the day when I was born."

"So you think this is a co incidence and something is connected?"

I said "Yes" sincerely.

"Oh! God! We humans, there is no bloody connections with that girl, there are no serendipities, there is nothing that is "Meant To Be," IT'S ALL IN OUR MIND. Remember this son, mind always play tricks on us in so many uncanny ways that you won't even know what it is really up to. So always remember **whatever you think is REAL, your thoughts are REAL but not TRUE**. When you know this thing well, you will be the happiest man in the world.

"Okay, I get it" I said without understanding a single word she said.

"So what do my cards mean" I asked her innocently.

"They simply mean you are here to kill time, you have no problem whatsoever and 20 min are up, give me my 20£ and I know I am right"

Humbled and disgraced I came out of that psycho's den. I mean, Come on! Whatever! But she was right I was there to kill time and I had no problem in my life whatsoever.

It was fun though; women they always surprise me no matter of what age they are; I guess they do surprise every man. Women can be anyone and anything but not a single thing a man think of. I went home and got into my bed. I thought of everything, literally everything from the woman I love to the Syria crisis. Finally, after 3hours my brain said "We are done thinking of everything so please sleep" I said "Alright" and slept.

My departure was near, I thought if I leave this magnificent country without defeating that bloody pigeon, how I could see myself for the rest of my life. So I decided that I am going to catch it even if it costs me all my saving. Which is very less by the way, but enough for that bloody pigeon, beer, pizza, shopping and roaming or whatever. I guess that's a lot of money, suddenly I realised I am a rich man. *Wow! I am a rich man, I mean I can buy anything I need, and that's all I needed in my life. God! I am thinking anything lately! This pigeon is driving me nuts for sure.*

So next day, I bought the trap worth 20 pound and set it in the balcony. It was like a mouse trap but a bit bigger. So I set the trap in the balcony. I left the bait inside the trap, a bowl of water and popcorn crumbs, yes, pigeons love popcorn crumbs.

After 3 days, in the evening the bird finally arrived and it was roaming around the cage. It was smart to know about the trap definitely. I went close. Fearlessly it was staring at me. Then on its right leg I saw the ring, the red ring and the code on it, "Gotcha!" I said. I went inside, got my phone took a pic, zoomed in and there was the code: **AERC 6884 09**.

I opened my laptop entered the code in the Lostpigeon section on homingpigeon.co.uk. It displayed the name of the owner & his details. James Burton was the owner of my trouble. I called him straightaway.

"Hello?" A deep dark voice answered.

"Hi, am I speaking to MR. James Burton."

"hmmm."

"Well, I found your pigeon."

"Do you mean Elena?"

"I don't know Elena, but I have the code. "The code is…?"

"AERC 6884 09?"

"Exactly" I approved.

"So did you catch her?"

"Almost, she is right in front of me and she will enter into the trap anytime soon."

"Haha, Elena won't get into that trap, she never did she never will, she is a racing queen. She has won lot of titles in her glory days, but now she is lost and she does NOT wish to come home. Many guys called up till now complaining she is troubling them, but no one could catch her."

"Ok…., what if she does fall into my trap. Will you come and collect it."

"Even if you do, I request you to bring her to me, I live in Maidenhead."

"I just live nearby in Slough, So will you come?"

"No Son, I am a retired old man, and a round trip to slough might cost me 20 pound."

"But it's your pigeeeeon you should take care of it. Even the website says that owner will come."

"You are right son, but she cannot be owned so I am not her owner. If you ever catch her, call me and then we will see what we can do."

"Okay be ready, I will catch her."

"Good luck mate."

"Remember son, **something cannot be possessed even though you own them**."

For Heaven's sake No Philosophy please, I expressed to heaven above.

"Thank You Mr Burton, let's see what happens" I hung up.

Elena was staring at me, now I have a name for her great! I was right all along she was a feminine.

Now we were staring at each other. I asserted her to get in the trap, but she simply flew away again. Disappointed, I went for my evening jog.

During my jog, I gave some grave thought to this entire fiasco, especially about Mr James, how can a man won't even care about pigeon who gave him honour & glory. Why he no longer cared for her, or did he cared for her so long that he gave up and finally accepted, that something cannot be possessed no matter what you do. Or was he a drunkard lost in his glory days. Let it go I thought I have my own problems, which I had no clue what they were.

It's been 7 days since the trap has been set and since that day I haven't seen Elena, I thought she was gone. I felt bad that I couldn't outwit her. I guess owner was right; Elena cannot be tamed, so I should accept the situation and move on with my life.

My last weekend in Europe was in Amsterdam, before leaving I made sure I leave enough of fresh water and Popcorn in the trap, anticipating she will be waiting in the trap when I return.

I came back from Amsterdam and the adventure which I had in that city, I have no recollection of it. Amsterdam does that to you. You have fun but magic mushrooms erases your memory. I came Monday morning and checked the trap first, it was empty like before. I was disappointed. I thought I should be happy that the bird is gone and not troubling me, but EGO is one crazy thing, it won't let you rest until you win or you are crushed completely.

All day I thought, then realised my intention were so wrong about Elena. Why was I after it her so madly, she was not even mine. I know she did trouble me, but not that much. In fact, that pigeon gave me something to live for. My last month was occupied because of the Elena. Actually, it helped me to kill time which I needed desperately. In the end, I felt gratitude for the bird. It was a blessing in disguise. I realised that I need to seek some real purpose in life rather wasting my life in such shallow chases. Elena, my enemy ripped me apart only to make me realise that there is more to life rather going around the things which are totally out of my control. Today is Elena, tomorrow maybe some girl after that maybe promotions, more money, bigger house etc. a never ending list of satisfying my EGO. Witch/Elena is nothing but my ego.

I came home spent the eve in the balcony. I wanted to see the bird one last time before I go but no luck… 4 days to take OFF.

Last night in London arrived, with my whiskey I was waiting for the bird, with every peg, drag of smoke my life in UK was approaching its conclusion and the hunt as well. It was fun overall I thought; despite all the hardship it was amusing. I said good night to UK and Elena and went to bed.

Last morning in UK was a bit nostalgic, I was waiting for this morning since last 60 days, but when it finally arrived I was not feeling good, I wanted to stay as well as leave. As usual, I have no recollection of when I packed my bag last night.

With heavy a heart, I made one last black coffee, I went into the balcony. Took my first sip of the coffee and I heard the noise. I knew it was her; I could hear her but could not see her. Then it struck me. I looked sideways.

Elena was tamed.

I was ecstatic, the bird enjoying the popcorn & water. I did a little victory dance, then it struck me; I have to return her to the owner, which was a hectic job. I was in dilemma, should I return her to the owner or should I let her be free, epic confusion. So decided I will open the cage and let her fly. So I opened the cage but the bird was still in "Come on be out now, the WAR IS OVER!! (I WIN ☺). I have nothing against you, go fly bird go fly."

In reply she said nothing.

I thought maybe I am scaring her that's the reason why she is not leaving, so I went in got ready for my last day in office, watched TV and checked luggage. 1 hour passed but the bird did not budge. So I went to the cage and pushed it. But answer was No, Elena found her new home. I was pissed, I mean now I wanted to set her free but she did not want to leave, what wrong I have done in my life to deserve this. Now I was supposed to leave for office and from there to airport. I was not coming back to check the bird what was I supposed to do, can't leave a bird into the cage. What if the cage door gets locked due to wind, the bird will DIE. Finally, I had to call Mr. James.

"Hi, Good Morning Mr. James."

"You caught her" He replied.

"Yes."

"Can you come and pick her up? it will be at my apartment's reception."

"No son, I can't, I am old and my legs don't have strength."

"So what am I supposed to do with her?"

"Either bring her to me or give her to the pigeon control office which is in central London."

"Central London? it is quite far away for me and it will be quite tough to carry the bird by London tube."

"Then bring her to me if possible. Otherwise, keep the cage open. She will fly someday."

"Okay, I will come to you text me your address." I hung up. *Was I too humble? I thought. Elena was not my problem and this man did not give a damn about the bird. I was under no moral obligation of delivering the bird to such an insensitive man.*

I guess wining turn people too humble and they start making promises filled with pride.

Now, I have to deliver a bird, carry the bird all the way to maidenhead from Hillingdon. This was around 20 miles.

So now I have my handbag, my laptop bag, my main luggage and ELENA. Never thought this would end like this.

So I took all the luggage caught a train to west Drayton from there bus to my office in Hillingdon, all along I could see people staring at me and Elena. Few of my familiar commuters asked me about Elena, I narrated the entire story for the first time.

I reached Office, receptionist reacted "Oh My God! You are not allowed to take that up."

"I know I am just keeping it here, I will take it away with me while leaving."

"Are you taking it to India? That is not allowed" she said.

"I know. I will deliver to its owner, before heading to airport."

"Okay let me check" she called her boss and explained the situation.

"Okay, you can keep it but on the backside of the office in front of car park."

"Okay, thanks" I said.

"But where did you find it?" she asked and I repeated the entire story for the second time.

I went to the backside of my office and kept the cage in front of car park. I started to walk away, then I turnaround came back to Elena and opened the cage, hoping for a goodbye.

I went inside the office everyone was in strange mood as I was leaving. During the break, I took them to Elena hoping she is not there, they all met her and they all really liked her. And I narrated the entire story for the third time.

I told them that I am taking a train to maidenhead in lunch to return her to the owner.

My colleague who enjoyed the pigeon story from start was really proud of me. She looked impressed by me for the first time. *She was impressed NOW?, when I was leaving this country.*

"We will go maidenhead, I will take my car" She said.

"Sure? its 20miles" I asked.

"It's okay; we don't have much work to do today as well" She replied.

"Okay, thanks a Lot."

12pm, we reached car park on the back side of the office. Unfortunately, when we reached Elena was still there.

"Let's Go!" my colleague cheered.

I took the cage put it on the backseat of the car and we rolled to write the final page in the story of Elena.

During our 40 min journey, we talked a lot; Elena listened patiently.

"I never thought you are such a soft hearted man" replied my colleague who was of my age gorgeous and unmarried.

"No, I am not."

"Seriously, you always express yourself as reckless guy, but you are very humble."

"We all are that way aren't we?" I questioned.

"Not that thing" She pointed Elena.

"Well you were the one who first said pigeon are so cute, how I can call them filthy bla bla bla."

"Well, I no longer think that way after what she has done to you" She answered.

"Nothing happened to me, it's a normal pigeon trouble, which is quite common in UK."

"Maybe.......whatever" She commented.

We reached finally to Mr James house, Thanks google⊠.

"Let's go!" I asked to my colleague."

"Sorry, I have to call someone."

"Okay." *When did she get a boyfriend? I thought. And thought of her having a boyfriend freaked me out for no reason. Heaven knows when I will get into my flight.*

It was a nice home, sorry can't describe it because this is a short story. But it was a nice typical British house.

I rang the bell.

A woman opened the Door. "Yes?"

"Hi, may I See Mr James Burton, I got his Elena" I said showing off Elena like a trophy.

"My My, finally, you are the one who brought long lost Elena, it's been 2 years since he is been waiting. OH! Sorry please come in. Please go inside, I followed her instruction and entered into the room. There was a man on the wheelchair with his eyes closed.

He was dead.

That's what I thought from the first look of his posture. I knocked on the open door.

He snapped and took a moment to resurrect, seeing Elena he said "Welcome, the Man Who captured Elena."

"But remember, though you possess it does not mean....

"You own it"...I continued.

"Quick learner you are."

"Here is your Elena."

"Please keep it on the bed, tell me about how you caught her."

I repeated the entire story for the fourth time.

"Well you are a man with determination; no one would do this, especially investing the money and all."

"Thanks" I blushed. *Finally, first time in my life somebody appreciated me.*

Silence.

So to break the silence, I said "I have to leave as I have to get back to the office."

"Wish you all the luck mate, I could have offered you a tea or whiskey but you are in hurry" said James.

"A double of whisky will do, I have 10 min for it for sure" I said.

"Ha-ha."

"Lily," he called, and the woman who opened the door to me arrived.

"Get a double for the gentleman. He deserves it."

"Sorry, we are out of whiskey" She answered.

"Who drank that?" he asked.

"You did, yesterday I told you that it was the last bottle. But you kept drinking."

"Oh! Now I remember."

"Sorry, mate. Tea, perhaps?"

"No, It's ok, I will take my leave."

I left his house feeling accomplished but it could have been icing on the cake if I had double of whisky. Never mind, I will have it in the flight.

I got in the car.

"You, Ok?" she asked.

"Yes, I win Elena loose."

"Haha, Winner Winner chicken dinner" she said.

"Yeah."

We reached office by 3 pm, still there was no work. To my No surprise all of my colleagues bought cake and Beer. We cut the cake, raised the toast to everyone & thanked everyone. Lots of laughs & gossip of last one year, they all said they are going to miss me a lot. Because the only lively man will be gone from a very serious office. Final Hugs, laugh, few tears and I lifted my bag it was 5 pm. 4 hours to take off.

"Okay then time to say goodbye chaps, see you someday. I need to catch the bus."

"I will drop you" replied my colleague.

"It's far"

"No worries, No worries" she said.

We got into the car and we headed for Heathrow airport, it was quite an emotional moment for me leaving the London office but I had to, as my job was done. In car there was uncanny silence, certainly we developed emotion over a year between us. It struck me, my colleague was bold, beautiful and exactly that sort of women I always wanted to marry. I dismissed the thought that I was in love with her. I decided, I will not tag that relation if it was friendship, love or complicated. It was just good.

Heathrow Airport 6 pm:

She stopped the car at drop off point. She said good bye with a long Hug, which made me confuse and uncomfortable.

She said "Good bye, hope you find the love of your life. If I ever come to India, I won't give you call, so don't expect." I said "OK, but I will give you a call if I ever come to back to UK."

"You will, your love is here" She smiled mischievously.

"Whooo?" I asked hesitantly.

"Your Elena, You fool! Now go don't make me ...."

"Goodbye, I will miss you" I said and turned around. God! I can never understand woman that's for sure and from now on I won't even attempt to.

I began to walk away from her towards the entrance, one thing life had taught me in such moment: Never ever look back, not even a little peek because these are the moments where we fall in love and we all know what happens afterwards.

Anyway, my mind was back to Elena victory. Happy I was. Happy I was. I got into plane I got window seat but adjacent to wings anyway at least better than middle seat.

10 min to take off, I was looking outside; it was summer in England the sun was still shining, a beautiful twilight. Staring outside the window, I murmured "Good bye England I am going to miss you."

And there came something flying. She settled herself on the airplane wings.

ELENA!!! I could see the red ring.

"No No No" I said loudly.

"Is everything ok sir? Asked the airhostess, *God! So much of make Up!*

"Yeah, everything is just fine, actually I have a question?"

"Yes?"

"Can you see Elena?"

"What?"

"Sorry, I mean can you see that Pigeon on that wing?"

She came close and she ducked a little, *God! Too much of Perfume*!

"Yes, it is very beautiful and what's the ring on her leg" She asked.

"I don't know" I said, "Now I no longer know anything."

"Excuse me?"

"Nothing, Thank you."

She left, giving me a strange look. As if I was some sort of pervert.

I called James.

"Mr. James."

"You still see her, don't you?" he said.

"Yes, she is on the wing of my plane. How do you know?" She flew away when I tried to feed her.

"It's your turn now, enjoy the following and remember they can travel to worlds end; INDIA is not a great distance for them."

"It can't be her, it's impossible."

"You will believe one day and remember the number AERC 6884 09. Best of luck! Have a safe trip" He hung up.

Plane began to take off Elena flew away. But somewhere in the corner of my mind I am afraid I will see Elena again. **THE END-is it?, I closed my eyes and the plane took off, hoping not to see Elena again.**

4

DRIVE...

Chapter 1: Nothing to loose

He was happy, driving a Porsche 911 Carrera 4S on the freeway. It did not belong to him; he was a salesman on his way to deliver the car to the mysterious old man.

Last Monday, a mysterious old man entered into the showroom, approached him and ordered "I want a Porsche 911 Carrera 4S." Oldman completed all the formalities instantly and this salesman sold a very costly car in a slack season. Everyone else thought he tricked old man to buy this model and got bonus by making big sale in the shortest time. Everyone asked him how he did it, he simply answered "It's a secret". He was not a fool to lose his bonus by telling the truth that he did absolutely nothing. Old man demanded car to be delivered at his Villa by Friday eve which was at the other end of the state. He also promised to do the necessary arrangements to drop the salesman back next morning.

So, here he was on a great drive of 250 miles along the coast line in a Porsche 911 his dream car and on his dream drive. Life could have never been so better he thought. He always got what he wanted, Always. He was a man of a very small dream now. He was from a well to do family and he achieved a lot in his life. He had a highly paid job in software security testing where he had to make sure that no one could hack or break the software. He achieved mastery in it at a very young age of 25 and wrote a book on it, which is now considered as bible in the security testing. He had many opportunities to travel the world because of the job thus helping him complete his bucket list. By the age of 27, his parents passed away in a car accident, they were proud parents. He had no sibling or relatives to look after. He loved only one woman all his life but things did not work out. She had high dreams so one fine morning she left without saying Goodbye. That was the only thing that ever bothered him. But he pretended that he had made peace with it as he realized no one gets a proper closure when it comes to relationships. After that he dated other women but fate always had other plan for women that came into his life. He unwillingly become a man where women can rest in his arms and fix their minds, then go their own way. He always wanted them to stay but things never worked out.

With lot of money and no one to spend it on, he began charity which attracted even more money. He realized an uncanny law of money; the more you let it flow away from you the more it will come to you, thus he was always a rich man. He donated half the money to charity and rest of the money was given to needy people who met him along the way.

After the departure of his love and parents he had very less to live for, he was quite alone but not lonely. He already proved to his peer and society that he was extra ordinary individual so even that end was conquered. He had no liability nor was he keen on getting married for indefinite time. Thus, at his career high and big salary he decided to call it a retirement. He was criticized by his peers and friends but he hardly cared.

He decided that he is going to live a simple life not aiming for money, stardom or whatever. He just wished to breathe through the life as all the goals have been conquered. So he made a decision that he will purposefully live common man's life, because that's what he missed all his life.

After quitting job, his plan was simple. Experiment with all the jobs in the world like fishing, key maker, pizza delivery boy, dishwasher in a restaurant, construction worker etc., he was a happy man living in the world whole heartily. And now there was another feather in his cap: driving a Porsche 911. He could have afforded this in the past but refrained from wasting money because his future was uncertain. So driving through the freeway he expressed gratitude to entire world for his wonderful life.

After a drive of 4 hours and following the map given to him by old man, he finally could see the distant villa located on the cliff quite away from the world. Google map were hardly of any use. Old man was right, his hand drawn map was the only way to reach Villa.

In twilight, he reached at top of the cliff and he could see a lighthouse right beside the villa. He wondered why would they need a lighthouse for a villa, he dismissed his question as he was no expert on the coast line. He approached the main gate which was guarded by 2 armed men with MP7's. One of the guards raised the hand and signalled him to stop though he was already standstill in front of gate. He looked at the camera which checked him intently in return and after a moment the gate opened. Guard did not pay heed towards the gate or the visitor. They approached and passed by him to check the road, making sure he was alone. He did not have a good feeling about this. His premonition warned him, he ignored this feeling, he convinced himself it was just a feeling, feelings are feelings they always go away, eventually.

He entered inside and he was wrong it was not a villa it was a palace, something so grand that he had not even seen in movies. He followed the road heading towards the palace. The entire vicinity was full of exotic gardens & fountains. He felt like entering into scenic painting. He followed path towards the palace he could hear the ocean slamming against the cliff & sun slowly disappearing in the air. The palace was almost a mile away from the main gate and he could see the entire place being protected by a huge wall except the seaside.

Chapter 2: The Girl.

Approaching the main door of palace, he could see a girl standing in white shirt and black skirt. He could not catch the complete glimpse till he pulled over his car in front of her. He got out of the car and approached the girl, before he could move his lips to speak, it was her. The only person he did not want to be there, his only nightmare, his only regret, his only love, his only nemesis.

"Hi" She said, she wanted to smile but she was overwhelmed with emotion.

"Hello, how are you?" he asked.

"I am fine" she said without a smile but her eyes were speaking a completely different story, there was guilt in her eyes he could see it.

"You look younger" he said with a smile.

"Thanks" she chocked.

"Where can I park this car, I am the salesman who is delivering this Car."

"Let it be there, I will take care of it" she stated.

"Here you are!" appeared the old man from behind.

He approached him and shook his hand; he did not even bother to see the car.

"Here is your car sir, all set to roll I have checked everything" he presented the key to the Oldman.

"I trust you, completely."

"Darling, will you please inform them to park it in the basement" asked the old man to the girl.

"I was just about to call the butler" she replied taking the keys.

"You are a Star" replied Old man.

"Please come in young man, she will take care of the car".

He took his backpack from the car followed the old man, wondering if the girl he loved was the old man's wife or worse his mistress. With heavy feet he reached inside the palace.

"This is most beautiful place I have seen, it is no less than heaven and I am quite honoured to do the delivery" he remarked.

"It is just a show off. Reality is happiness and happiness is gratitude."

"Even I am a firm believer in gratitude" he replied.

"Are you?" asked the old man, "how come?"

"I do not know how, but things start coming to you once we are thank full of whatever we have. Gratitude is like a dinner host. It wants you to have more food even though you are full."

"Nice way of putting it" laughed old man. "Even I started with a small business and I was happy. Though it was a small business, I was grateful for at least 15-20 times' a day. I was rewarded more and more as I believed in the gratitude and empathy."

"Sorry, what would you like to have? Tea, coffee or anything?" asked the old man realizing he has missed the basic courtesy.

"Just water and I shall take my leave if that is possible for you. I know you promised me that you will drop me next morning but…." He asked hesitantly.

"Actually, I could have dropped you now but after our short discussion on the gratitude, I would really like to have a drink with you. You look like an interesting man. Please, I Insist you to stay, your safety will be my responsibility" mocked old man.

"No, it is nothing like that I am an ordinary man. This grand place is making me nervous" he replied.

"Do not be. Please I insist you to stay for tonight, my secretary has done all the arrangements for you already" asserted old man.

"You mean the lady who received me?" He asked hoping for a 'yes' reply.

"Yes. She looks after this palace and management. It is a shame it will be her last night. She is switching the job and moving to Rome, Vatican City to be precise. She will look after Vatican museum."

"That's great." He replied.

"Yes, she is very good in management. I offered her thrice the money than romans, but she denied. She said it's not about money but her love. Love stories, they all are the same, driven more by ego than love. People just can't take it when someone does not love them back. Her story is sort of same; I decided not to get into it. Never mind! So will you please stay tonight, after long time I am having conversation with someone and you look like someone I can talk to."

He was relieved and ready to stay as he realised she was not his wife or lover. Plus, he might get a chance to know about her recent development. If she is willing to speak he might get some closure helping him to kill his only surviving regret, his only ghost which is still haunting him somewhere in the corner of his mind.

"Are you sure?" he smiled.

"I insist" answered old man.

"Allright!" He said.

"Excellent!" clapped old man and called the butler.

"Please take our guest to the guestroom facing the seaside and take care of him properly." "Sure Sir" replied the butler.

"It's now 6; take some rest young man. We will meet by 8 over dinner. I have some business to take care of, so see you at dinner. If anything is needed, please let us know."

"Thanks."

Butler was a silent man, he led him up through the stairs and towards his room. He entered the room. He immediately wanted to get out of it. He did not like too much of fancy & beautiful stuff. But he had no other option but to stay, he craved closure.

He checked the stunning view of sea from the balcony. He caught himself asking too many questions regarding the current situation. Her presence has disturbed him for sure. He decided to clear his mind with a shower but instead he ended up thinking of all the conversation he might have with her. He thought of complaining but then finally decided to go silent as he had no rights over her. Their story ended 2 years back. She was on her way to Vatican for some joker so why should he bother. He decided that he would do banal talks and won't talk of anything that will lead to their past. He even doubted her presence at this place, considering if this was some sort of trap as he never believed in co-incidences.

Chapter 3: The dinner

After an hour of sea gazing, he came to the conclusion that the old man's is thinking of offering the job to him as the replacement of his current secretory, otherwise why would he take such efforts for him?

He got ready, he had no fancy clothes. He wore casual white shirt and denim jeans. He reached the dining. It was decorated with lot of food. He hated such sort of dinner, where often food is wasted. Both of them have already taken their seat and were discussing business. As he approached dining table, they rose & exchanged greetings.

"Sorry, I am not well dressed; I never expected it to be so beautiful" he added. "It's okay" said the old man "please take the seat"

"What would you like to drink?" asked the old man.

"A beer would be fine" he answered

"Lady was right about you" expressed the old man with delight "Budweiser I guess."

"Yes."

"She told me about your taste, also she told me how you guys departed due to unusual circumstances." said old man.

"I would rather say unusual people lead to departure, circumstances were just fine" he snapped and regretted.

Old man smiled, girl ignored his statement.

"So you cannot eat much when there is variety of food on the table?" asked the old man

"Yes, she informed you rightly. She has a good memory. Can I ask you something?" He questioned.

"Sure son."

"What do you do for living?"

"I deal in population stats, this place is my office as well. I handle software which maps population of earth and highlights when things go way up or way down, it is us who provide the exact data of human population to WHO (World Health Organization). More importantly, this place is not owned by me. I am just a chief in charge officer here."

"OH" he exclaimed.

"Yes son I am not a rich man as you think" smiled old man.

"No, No I did not mean that, okay yeah, I thought that" he smiled and all of them laughed.

"Honesty! I chose the right guy to dine with me" Continued Old man "But it is a highly paid job and I am on the verge of retirement by next year, so the company has given me Porsche 911 as a retirement gift in advance. Thanks to her, she looked after everything since last year. It's sad that it is her last night that's why we have prepared all of her favourite food, Not for you" mocked the old man.

"So what's your story" asked the old man.

"My story is sort of weird and some people call me lazy or a man with very low ambitions, Some think I have no future, some even called me modern crazy saint..." he narrated his entire life story, they listened very intently. He also mentioned her quite briefly in his life span, he appreciated her & gave her credit for his success."

"Great! Now that's a way to live life, so what's your next plan" Asked the Old man.

"Honestly, all I plan is to go home tomorrow morning. I live a one day at a time, from my viewpoint that's the only way to live life. I firmly believe that life is senseless, no matter how hard you try you cannot map it out. No matter what you achieve there will always be a WHAT'S NEXT?"

"You have some philosophy."

"What do you think of death" asked the host.

Taken aback by the question throwing a quick glance at her, he continued "I think it is the most beautiful thing on the planet, I have no clue why people take it very negatively. As Oscar Wilde quoted "Death must be so beautiful. To lie in the soft brown earth, with the grasses waving above one's head, and listen to silence. To have no yesterday, and no to-morrow. To forget time, to forget life, to be at peace.

"Brilliant! that's my favourite as well."

Dinner continued for another 2 hours all were lost in conversation until it was 10 pm.

"You were right, he is great in conversation and he has heck of knowledge of world" commented the old man at the end of the dinner.

"I must retire now. I have a 4 am flight. ROMA! Calling!" She smiled.

"Sure" answered old man.

"Thank you so much for a lovely dinner sir. It was awesome."

They all left the dinner table. Old man said, "I have work to attend, so wake me up before you leave."

"Sure I will." she smiled

"Thank you it was one of the best dinner I ever had" he added.

"My pleasure" replied Old man and left leaving them alone.

Chapter: 4 Dead silence.

"So, How you been?" he asked after a long pause

"Perfect" she smiled.

"Still won't say a word, about how messed up you are, always showing stuff which are not there and never letting anyone in" he smirked.

"You know, that's how I am" she answered.

"Yeah, I know" he answered.

"Seems like you are living a dream" she asked.

"Yeah, I can't complain." He answered.

"I am glad for you that you are heading ROMA, you always wanted to go there right?"

"Yes" She smiled.

The discussion continued and later they took a walk along the cliff under the moonlight laughing and recalling old days until it was 1 am.

"Time has come, that I should say goodbye. I am so sorry that I could not say goodbye before leaving us. I was too scared and I knew if I was there in your life you would have not achieve anything because you were too much in love with me." she sobbed weakly.

He smiled "Your assumptions are wrong, anyway from your angle they will always be right, so why discuss this now? I am glad that your life turned out quite well, best of luck"

She smiled "let's go."

They headed back to palace. She got ready packed her bags, knocked on Old man's room. They escorted her to cab, she hugged old man and thanked for all the things he had done for her.

She approached him. "Good bye, I am sorry the way I disappeared, I could have at least said goodbye, but you knew how crazy I was" she hugged and kissed him goodbye.

He smiled "goodbye".

She left.

Old man watched the ending of this love story with a delight and said "Catch some sleep young man. We will meet at the breakfast."

"Nope, I am too ecstatic to sleep"

"How about some coffee?" offered Oldman.

"Sure."

Chapter: 5: 7 Reasons to Die

He followed Old man to the kitchen where old man prepared coffee discussing closure in the relationships and how the salesman must be liberated, to move forward in his life. He agreed and accepted the coffee by the old man. Old man led him to porch where they sat facing the moonlight, beach and the lighthouse

"It is quite beautiful out here" he said "you must be feeling quite lucky to live at such a place."

Ignoring his remark old man asked "I asked you a question regarding the death remember?"

"Yes, I do remember" answered the salesman.

"You are a man with lot of experience and knowledge of how our beautiful but stupid world works. Have you ever wondered why people die? What is the reason behind their death? Of course aging, natural calamities, accident, diseases are the ways to die, but these are not the reasons."

"I thought about it but sometimes I felt that logic behind it is quite uncertain and bewildering. However, somewhere in the corner of mind I always thought there is a pattern. No one dies for no reason, like I wondered in few cases."

"Like?" asked curious old man.

"My parents, they were done with their life they were satisfied with what they have accomplished in their life. I was highly successful and they personally have achieved everything. There could have never been a better time for them to die, I may sound insane but…"

"Not at All son, Not at All, your analysis is almost perfect but there is a deeper reason for them to die to which I will come later."

"A deeper reason?"

"Son, I have been working with population stats, number of people die and born every year so basically been dealing in death and life all my life. This led to some deep observation regarding the death of a person. So as per my knowledge the death is categorized into 7 different types.

"That sounds interesting. What are those?" he asked.

"First is **The Achievers.** These are the people who have done a lot in their life and there is no role left for them to play nor anything that's left to go forward to. These are the people who crossed their finish line in the desired way plus average life expectancy comes into play simultaneously. Thus they are released. However, catch is it should not impact others, in negative way. Dying is normal but its repercussion can be devastating to others. So these fall into the category where everything is done and their death would not affect the world or people around them negatively.

"So do you mean that my parents were of this category?"

"I will tell you all the possible reasons of death and you choose which fits your parents"

"All right! What about your parents?" he asked

"I am an orphan" continued old man "I have never seen my parents. My parents died in an accident when I was 3 months old. I was raised by my uncle and aunt who were childless. They raised me like their own son but they always made sure that I was self-dependent. They were happy. Because of me they got the sense of purpose. I came into their life when they were on the verge of divorce. My aunt was going through depression as she was childless. I came into their life and it changed everything. They did well in their life. Later they did a lot of charity and welfare for orphans. Thus, my parent's death was actually a good event if we think in larger picture. A decade back even uncle passed away followed by aunt. They had done enough for the world, they were liberated, they were the achievers.

"But this can be applicable to anyone, what makes them special? If we see it this way then everyone has sort of achieved something." He asked

"Not necessary, death of my uncle and aunt did not matter to anyone, because they had done enough and overall they were happy about their life. I could see the sense of fulfilment in their last days. Nothing on the planet can be more fulfilling by timely and non-suffering death."

"But their death must have impacted you?"

"Yes it did. Like you, I thought it was a perfect time. After their departure, things went terribly wrong with my life, I almost went insane. I am quite thankful that they have not seen the worst phase of my life."

"Insane??"

"Nothing much. A typical story of bad marriage, alcohol addiction, drug abuse and terrible loneliness which was later sorted but it took around 10 years for me to get back into my senses"

"It must have been a great suffering for you?"

"In retrospect, not much. Everything goes away with time, emotions turn into memories and memories turn into data, data turns into small fragment of your life, that's the beauty of life. It always nullifies everything. Good nullifies bad, good luck nullifies bad luck. But the word suffering takes me to the next type.

"The Sufferers:

These are fine individuals who unfortunately land up in a wrong company or place and they cannot escape it. Due to system's wrong insertion they find themselves stuck with the evil people that death is their only way out. They are caught in the black hole due to systems fault. These are individuals who have absolutely no clue what is wrong; little do they know that it is not their fault. They are great but due to people around them they end up in a deep abyss of darkness. Chance is offered to them to get out of the loop but they decide to suffer for their loved ones. From the humanity view point, they are right but their suffering gets inevitable day by day. System does try to pull them out of mess but things are so interconnected that sometimes death is their only salvation.

We are placed here in this life to have a ball. Everything is possible and everything is achievable. But we humans lose so much in self obsession and vanity that we lose the track of life. These sufferers might die through agony all their life, system just grants them salvation and save them from the eternity of hell. Personally, my heart goes out for such beautiful individuals but their liberation is at least some consolation.

"But is it not unfair?" asked the salesman

"Life is unfair, Death is not. Death is for one's own good."

Watching salesman thinking, Old man asked "seems like you have an example, in your life for this category?"

"My friend was an angel but she chose a very wrong man to get married, he was an addict of all the things. She thought she could change him but she suffered and suffered. We all offered her help and begged her to get away from that man, but she refused. Finally, one night her husband accidently hit her and she died. Honestly, I was happy that she died."

"Excellent example, there are lot many women stuck in such situation. Liberation is the only solution; her death was the best thing ever happened to her."

"But I have a question. What about mentally retarded people, they are suffering as well" he asked.

"True but in most cases they are unaware that they are suffering and also it gives their parents a reason to live & love unconditionally. Nothing can be greater than unconditional love. That's what makes us human, unconditional love is the core entity of human evolution"

"As per my theory next comes the

The Hopeless:

"These are nothing but useless people which have no future **and** after knowing their characteristics it can be predicted that they are not going to make even a shred of significance on earth. They do not even affect other people in good way or bad way. They are so dumb **and** hopeless that their existence is mere trash on earth.

These individuals are most tough to find. To find someone who does not add anything to the society or economy is not easy. These are usually the rich men's screwed kids who usually die due to drug over dose or drunk car accident. I feel no pity for such sort of death but one thing is for sure they are rare. That's why death rate is lowest for this category."

"But they are humans. You cannot call them useless **and** expect them to die." He rebelled.

"True. Earth is all about fighting for existence and moving forward. These individuals are doing nothing. Everything should have a momentum. If we take currency; it is still intact because it flows. Even only those relationships last long where both individual are moving ahead in their life and adapting the constant change, relationships are bound to move ahead and come across new stages and they should flow with the course. People do not want to move nor want to accept the new stages in the relationship, thus their laziness turns the relation stale and it gets over. Put it in a very simple words "Stopping is dying".

"World has to flow in an order. Let's say for an example we all turn saints. We start living only for need and not for greed. If everyone is living happily; imagine how the world would survive? We won't need that many police or huge armies. We won't need fancy clothes, mobiles, laptop, drinks, smoke etc. 80% of the industries on the planet would shut down and the world might collapse, I am not saying all will die. Everything will be so plain and simple that people will no longer have any surprises, no colours, no happiness, no sadness, no drama no action, imagine can world especially human survive this? Today world can afford only few thinkers, few saints; few special ones.

That's why Useless people are not tolerated. I am not saying they are bad. They are anchors in human evolution."

"All right, it is an interesting theory that if the world will be perfect place it will not last long, I will indeed give it a thought."What is the next category?" asked salesman.

"The Medium

These people cannot be judged as good or evil but their death certainly can change life of people around them. Like death of important person in the family like father / mother or both, when their children are young. This type of death is a nightmare for a family but 1 death can lead to 3 or more better lives. Their life partner and children become more serious about their life; they start learning things early. Like my parents were Medium, because of their death I came into my uncle and aunt's life. They did a lot of charity, looked after orphans. They did service for others and later even I did a lot to make this world a better place."

"So you mean to say sometimes we have to kill a few to make other do what we or a system wants to do?"

"Yes"

"Is it not cruel and ruthless?" he asked.

"It is, no doubt but people have to die and there should be a protocol for it. We humans are evolving with each passing day. We are getting more logical and less emotional. Look at your generation; you feel less love, less parental responsibilities, less empathy. I am looking at the world from a top view and I am trying to normalize things. The way things are going we will eventually become completely logical which might lead to less harm or destruction in the world but it MIGHT also take out passion, love and empathy which are the core human entity.

"So you mean to say, children should have bad childhood, to do better in future life, so that they can take this world to the next level as they have become tough & Sensible."

"Sort of yes but death rate of the medium is very less compared to others, system hates to do that but it has to it sometimes. Well it is not necessary that the children around the medium will turn out good they can even turn into the most evil creatures on the planet."

"What you mean by the "system"? Do you mean god."

"God, system they all are one and the same, this term means: Things beyond normal beings control."

"All right, so people should die because they won't do anything special in their life and their death can lead to chain reaction which can help an individual to get on track?"

"Exactly."

"What can I say then, what is the next type?" He was convinced that he was talking to a madman.

"The Imposter

Most fascinating are the people who are imposters, they are good and evil at the same time. They are changing every day or they play a role of evil so long and after they turn to saint or vice versa which is unaccepted"

"What you mean unaccepted?"

I will tell you my experience; I had one of my friend who was a criminal. He created lot of trouble till his 30s and then something hit him. No one knew what happened but he surrendered to law. He completed his sentence came out of jail and after 7 days he died of accident. ACCIDENT, A perfect murder by nature.

"Even I heard lot of cases where addict, criminal or vindictive people turn their ways but that did not end well for them. As you seem expert in death what you think? why this happens?"

"Unpredictability, System hates it most as it breaks the very pattern of our survival. Everything needs a proper pattern so that things can be streamlined. For example, we humans always want a pattern so that we can plan and move ahead in life and actually we humans hate surprises when they are not in their favour, Same goes with the system. Imposters are the unpleasant surprise for the system."

"All right then why do Bad people live longer than Good people?" He asked

"That brings us to the next category" replied old man.

"The Bad men

See the thing with evil men is they generate lot of jobs. It's quite tough to take them out, unless they turn completely hopeless and they suffer. For example, terrorism generates lot of employment in those countries where it does not have other modes of earning. Also, Drugs, alcohol, human trafficking these are big money holders in the world's economy. Take them out and you will see the economy crash. In reality, World is a funny place and money can buy you everything. Even a LIFE.

"So you mean to say it is a necessary evil."

"Yes. See most important thing to run this world is the flow of currency. That you agree?

"Yeah."

"What makes you spend the money?"

"Anything can make me spend money" he answered.

"Yes grocery and household of course affordable by anyone. That comes under need section but NOT greed. But think, what makes the whole world run is the sorrow. Yes, sorrow, if this world would have been happy place it would have perished a long time back. Like, I mentioned before 'if everyone goes saint'. If you look through your life you have spent more when you were sad compared to when you were happy. Even Songs, if you listen majority of them are sad. It is quite funny that only 10% of the songs in this world are about happiness or feeling good. It is quite simple, when men go sad they go drinking and when women go sad they go shopping and these are of course the biggest industries."

"What it has to do with your theory of death?"

"Well, we need people to hurt people so that they can spend more & more money. Things like diamond, exotic dinner, dream house these have been sewn so deeply into the minds of society that we humans have to do it and if don't then we are stamped as a big loser. We will always have people around us that will be telling you how stupid and a big failure you are, thus this pressurizes you to buy stuff which can be anything from car to curtains though it is not needed.

Evil individual is anyone who creates the pressure on their peers by boasting about their achievement and treating others as their inferiors. Because at some point they were also treated inferior by other. This sense of Inferiority creates hunger for success and Success = Spending. There is a simple difference between good and evil. Whatever you have let it be a car, a beautiful wife, house or anything, if you make people feel around you that they do not have that and if some how you manage to hurt their esteem or ego. Then you are evil. Vanity is evil, rest everything is good & can be forgiven. But this as well is necessary otherwise how world economy would work.

"In this sense, we all are evil."

"Exactly, very true. We played evil part in someone else's life knowingly or unknowingly. But if you are doing consistently and knowingly all your life, that's pure evil; those are your bad men. They can do anything for money so that they can prove others their greatness, they won't mind killing, they won't mind harassing. They simply want attention and the best way to grab attention is Money.

They will always live long but this does not mean they will not suffer. They will live for so long that their own life becomes prison. When they run their course, they will still live to pay for their Karma. Heaven and Hell both are on earth you do not need to die to feel them.

"So, if I understand the theory of death by you. If one keeps adding to the society or economy one will live longer, no matter what you do. The more you help this world to move forward more are your survival chances. So all in all, you are trying to say is that; death is not in the hand of fate but actually it lies in one's deed."

"You are conversing my theory. But from your view point, you found ways to survive and I found ways to die."

"So what you expect from me" Asked the irritated salesman as this conversation was getting more and more unrealistic for him.

"What you think of this theory?" asked the Old man.

"I think it is good but it is vague it cannot be applied to every one's death. Of course it is quite imaginative and well researched but I do not think that there can be any truth to it. Death is written and it is in the hands of fate. So honestly this theory is average. Because we can always draw conclusion after someone dies but not before they die.

"What if I tell you that we need to draw conclusion before anyone dies, once conclusion is drawn then only the person dies."

"Then I would say this theory can have some substance but again how will one do it? It must need god, in fact lot of gods to capture the data and every detail of it"

"What if I say there are easier ways?" answered old man.

"What you mean?"

"We do not need gods, maybe there is no god."

"I do not understand."

"Come with me" said old man.

He got up and led him towards the light house which was almost 500m from the palace; he followed the old man through the meadows. It was almost dawn he could see the crimson shade in the sky. He was not sure what was happening but he had to know, so followed the old man without questioning. They reached light house. Old man placed his hand on the biometrics. The door opened. The door led to immediate up stair and downstairs. They went down.

They descended 3 stories down until they reached firm basement. It was dark. Old man disappeared into the darkness. He followed him but lost his track before he could call...

He heard Clapping noise.

Entire basement was lit, white lights and screens. All the walls were filled with the screen. With various people and their life displayed on the screen as if it was the live coverage of the entire world.

"What is all this?" he asked.

"Cases, of the people who might die soon if they fit into one of 7 categories."

"And you kill them?"

"Nope we let them die on time. Thus, they are freed from daily cliché of life. Like 2 individuals decide when a life should come in this world in the same way we humans also decided who should leave the world."

"This is crazy this cannot be real" he checked all the screen if they were real but he did not want to believe. "How can I believe it? This may all be made up."

"We can observe them, all of them."

Old man pulled out his cell phone and pushed buttons. Screen displayed salesman's entire data on the screens. He pulled in camera footage of his life since childhood. He then switched the cases from his love, his friends, family. He even displayed all the famous personalities and their life. Salesman named any person and the old man displayed the data.

He had no choice but to believe it.

"You are nothing but a murderer."

If a soldier kills for the country, he becomes a HERO. We are killing for earth we cannot be murderers.

"You are No GOD!"

"I may not be, but this job is carried out since the beginning, it was tough previously but technology has made it simpler."

"So you mean you belong to some sort of elite group which decides who lives and who dies."

"Nope, we decide only who dies" replied old man.

Shocked and first time intently thinking of old man's Theory of Death, "So if I sum up entire theory" He continued.

"The world needs sorrow so that financial flow can be intact. We have whole bunch of people that will make sure that most of the humans are sad. So humans can spend more and more money. We cannot kill endorser of sorrows because that's how economy works. But what world truly needs are the sets of extra ordinary individuals, which takes us to the new level of human evolution and whoever is not contributing they will be taken out and those who can contribute by their death will also be taken out. So as per your theory there are laws of death. World is designed preliminarily around 5%, of the people that can help remaining 95% of people to progress. Like scientists, innovators. And to make them special one's people around may die. For rest of 95% population a loop is created so that they can set a stage for extra ordinary individuals, anyone can choose to be in 5% or in 95% but they should be willing to prove themselves and to provide them a push; Death ALSO comes into play to motivate them."

"Excellent!....."

"Hold on! You said there are 7 categories but you informed me only about 6. The achievers, mediums, sufferers, Bad Men's, hopeless and The Imposter."

"You are right! I have not told you about the last category."

Chapter 6: THE RECRUIT

"It is me, is it not? The 7th Category" Grunted the salesman.

Old Man smiled. "Yes, The recruit."

"I made your wishes come true, only remaining were Porsche and the closure from her. That was the reason she was here last night. You can now live your life without regret and baggage's. You are now liberated to do a greater good"

"Does she know about this death business?"

"No."

"Is she alive and well?"

"Yes."

"My parents were killed because you wanted me here. They were mediums just like your parent, they were not achievers."

"Yes, but remember we did not made you what you are today, it was all your decision. We can add little push through circumstances but rest is in the hand of every individual. We are always what we chose. You chose this, the way you lived your life you made it till here."

"What you want me to do exactly?"

"Take my place and make this world a better place."

"No, I cannot do that I am not a killer."

"That's why I chose you."

"We do not want killers or psychopaths over here, we want men with moral values and good sense of predictability. You are the perfect candidate for it."

"So will you take this offer, I will teach you everything?"

"How this thing works?"

"System will pick up cases as per algorithm, data is acquired for every individual and then their cases will pop up in the system. You study the person, go through the depth of their life and conclude if they are worth dying. If you select them all you have to do is push the button, rest everything will be taken care off. It might sound easy right now but it takes around a year to get perfect in it."

"What if I do the job for some time and realize that it is not my cup of tea?"

"Then you will be relived from this troublesome life."

"What if I commit mistake?"

"Killing someone is not easy son, you will think twice before pushing the button. So do not worry you will be just fine."

"And what if I go out and tell everyone what is happening in this slaughterhouse?"

"You will be killed instantly and no one would actually believe you."

"Accept or reject, I am a dead man, am I not? I cannot go back to the world because I know too much. Whenever I will die; my category will be of recruit."

"Yes."

"Let's do it, then. I am IN."

The End.

If you have queries, feedback or Reviews
Please,
Drop a note
at
Sid.patki@outlook.com

Printed in the United States
By Bookmasters